BLACK BOY JOY

EDITED BY KWAME MBALIA

STORIES BY:

B. B. ALSTON

DEAN ATTA

P. DJÈLÍ CLARK

JAY COLES

JERRY CRAFT

LAMAR GILES

DON P. HOOPER

GEORGE M. JOHNSON

VARIAN JOHNSON

KWAME MBALIA

SUYI DAVIES OKUNGBOWA

TOCHI ONYEBUCHI

JULIAN RANDALL

JASON REYNOLDS

JUSTIN A. REYNOLDS

DAVAUN SANDERS

JULIAN WINTERS

BLACK BOY JOY

DELACORTE PRESS

Text copyright © 2021 by Kwame Mbalia
"The McCoy Game" © 2021 by B. B. Alston
"Extinct" © 2021 by Dean Atta
"Epic Venture" © 2021 by Jay Coles
"Percival and the Jab" © 2021 by P. Djèlí Clark
"Embracing My Black Boy Joy" © 2021 by Jerry Craft
"There's Going to Be a Fight in the Cafeteria on Friday and You Better Not Bring Batman"
© 2021 by Lamar Giles
"Got Me a Jet Pack" © 2021 by Don P. Hooper
"The Gender Reveal" © 2021 by George M. Johnson
"The Definition of Cool" © 2021 by Varian Johnson
"The Griot of Grover Street" © 2021 by Kwame Mbalia
"Five Thousand Light-Years to Home" © 2021 by Suyi Davies Okungbowa
"Coping" © 2021 by Tochi Onyebuchi
"But Also, Jazz" © 2021 by Julian Randall
"First-Day Fly" © 2021 by Jason Reynolds
"Our Dill" © 2021 by justin a. reynolds
"Kassius's Foolproof Guide to Losing the Turkey Bowl" © 2021 by DaVaun Sanders
"The Legendary Lawrence Cobbler" © 2021 by Julian Winters
Jacket art copyright © 2021 by Kadir Nelson

All rights reserved. Published in the United States by Delacorte Press, an imprint of Random House Children's Books, a division of Penguin Random House LLC, New York.

Delacorte Press is a registered trademark and the colophon is a trademark of Penguin Random House LLC.

Visit us on the Web! rhcbooks.com

Educators and librarians, for a variety of teaching tools, visit us at RHTeachersLibrarians.com

Library of Congress Cataloging-in-Publication Data is available upon request.
ISBN 978-0-593-37993-6 (trade) — ISBN 978-0-593-37994-3 (lib. bdg.) —
ISBN 978-0-593-37995-0 (ebook)

The text of this book is set in 12.5-point Sabon MT Pro.
Interior design by Jen Valero

Printed in the United States of America
10 9 8 7 6 5 4 3 2
First Edition

TO THE ONES THEY CALLED ANGRY, BROKEN, SAD, AND HOPELESS, BUT WERE SILENT AMIDST YOUR JOY

CONTENTS

INTRODUCTION

Here's a secret: I don't like watching the news. Is that weird? It's because for a long time, when I would come into the kitchen for my fifth snack in thirty minutes and my parents had the television on, the news was always reporting on some local shooting or some death or some other tragedy that made my mother shake her head and my father scowl at the screen. Because nine times out of ten, a face like mine was on the screen.

Here's another secret: when I'm happy I cry. Happy for myself, happy for my friends, happy for some stranger who just won a lifetime supply of string cheese—it doesn't matter; I will tear up as I'm jumping up and down in excitement.

One more secret: I want you to be happy.

Okay, that one wasn't really a secret but it had to be said, so just pretend with me, okay? And as long as we're pretending, imagine me dumping those three secrets into a giant bowl, inviting sixteen Black author friends to help me stir while they add in a dollop of magic and a sprinkle of swag, and what do we get?

Black Boy Joy.

The term was coined back in 2016 by Danielle Young and has grown to encompass the revelry, the excitement, the sheer fun of growing up as boys in and out of the hood. Their stories—our stories—deserve to be highlighted on the afternoon news. Explored. Seen and celebrated. I am thrilled that this book brings together so many different types of these stories from so many incredible authors.

So sit back. Grab your string cheese. Prepare to laugh, cry, and maybe even dance, but most of all, prepare to feel joyful.

THE GRIOT OF GROVER STREET

BY KWAME MBALIA

PART ONE

HOMEGOING. That's what Fort's mother and Aunt Jess and Mimi called it. Homegoing. Sounded fun, actually, like returning to your own bedroom after sleeping over your cousin's house for a week. Or a party at three p.m. every day when school let out to celebrate being done with classes. That would've been cool. But homegoing meant something different.

It meant a funeral.

The church marquee read ANTOINETTE ROBINSON'S HOMEGOING, FRIDAY 5:30 P.M., and it was wrong. Nobody knew an Antoinette Robinson—they called her Aunt Netta. She had the warmest hugs, the biggest smiles, and the sweetest apple turnovers Fort Jones had ever tasted, which she dusted with sugar and served after church services at the repast.

Fort would miss the turnovers, not because they were delicious (they were) or because she made one special for him when he couldn't sit still during the sermon and got sent to the kitchen to help (she always had one set aside), but because as he sat there kicking his feet and eating the hot, sticky dessert, Aunt Netta would sing.

He'd miss the singing too.

That's what Fort was thinking about when the strange old man appeared in front of him like magic. There Fort was, running out the Grover Street Church's double doors into the Carolina sun, sprinting through the parking lot to the grassy field on the other side, cuffing the tears out his eyes, when the man materialized out of nowhere. Fort almost managed to pull up and sidestep to the left.

CRASH

Suddenly down was up, left was right, his knee throbbed painfully, and Fort tasted the delightful flavor of dirt. Crunchy dirt. He was going to have to brush his teeth for an hour to get the taste out. But as he lay on his back staring up at the sky thinking of the amount of mouthwash he'd need, he heard the strangest thing. Words, yes, but strung together like he'd never heard before.

"The lightning! Spilled the lightning! And the fireflies, oh, they'll be angry. Hmm, is that—Oh, biscuits! The chuckle-snorts!"

Fort sat up to find the strange old man on his knees,

digging through an overturned wagon with the saddest expression. And if that wasn't weird enough, the man's outfit was. He wore a long cape—black on the outside, purple on the inside—silver pants, mismatched flip-flops with the tag still attached, and, to top it all off, a yellow derby hat with a white feather, the words "Gary the Griot" stenciled on the brim.

Fort gawked at him, but when the man finally looked up and their eyes met, the boy hurried to help.

"Sorry!" Fort said. "I didn't see you. I was . . . well, I wasn't paying attention." He didn't want to mention the tears or the reason behind them. Why did there have to be so much sadness in the world? But before the corners of his eyes could prickle all over again, Fort spotted a humongous glass jar tilted on its side and frowned.

"Happens to the best of us at the worst of times," the old man said. "Apology accepted. I'm sure you didn't— OH, BISCUITS, THE JOY IS GONE!" He reached down and grunted and heaved the jar into the air, studying a giant crack that ran along the bottom.

Actually, maybe humongous was an understatement.

The jar came up to Fort's waist, and he was tall for his eleven years. And not only was it big, it was wide as well, so wide that Fort struggled to understand how it could have fit inside the wagon with the rest of the stuff in the first place. The glass was stained blue, so much so that it looked like it used to hold blue raspberry Kool-Aid.

"The joy, the joy! It's gone! My last delivery, gone!" The man waved his arms in the air—which should've been impossible because he still held the jar—in dismay.

Fort went to dust himself off, then tried not to groan as his hands came away wet and stained. He was going to be in so much trouble. Bad enough he'd left the church in the middle of the service, crying like a toddler, but now this. His one good suit (he was getting too big for it; his ankles were peeking out from under his cuffs) was covered in that blue stuff, and . . . what *was* it?

"I'm so sorry. This is all my fault," Fort apologized. "I was—"

"FORTITUDE JONES, WHAT ARE YOU DOING?"

Uh-oh.

Mama's voice was so sharp it could cut glass. As Fort turned to see her marching down the stairs—her black dress and black shawl fluttering in the summer breeze, one hand on her back, one hand on her rounded stomach, one week away from her due date—he braced for the tongue lashing sure to come. This wasn't the first time he'd gotten in trouble at church, and it wouldn't be the last.

So when she stepped past him to help the strange man, Fort was confused.

"Are you okay, Mr. G?" Mama asked.

Did she know this guy?

The strange old man, still struggling under the weight of the giant cracked jar, waddled around to face her and tried to bow. "Of course, Madam Jones, it was but an accident."

At least, that's what Fort thought he tried to say. But the man, Mr. G, had his face smushed against the bottom of the jar, so what it sounded like was "Offacoursh, bagabones, lizard butt dragon lint." It was so preposterous that Fort started to smile, which of course was the exact moment when Mama whirled around and laid into him.

"Fortitude Jones, how many times have I told you to watch where you're going? You get so excited you don't look but two feet in front of you. Did you apologize?"

"Yes, Mama," Fort said, but for good measure he turned to Mr. G and did so again. "Sorry for knocking over all your stuff."

Mr. G sighed and flapped a hand (nearly dropping the jar—Fort was starting to get concerned). "No worries, young man, provided, of course"—Mr. G waddled over and peered at the boy from beneath a pair of impressively bushy eyebrows, which looked like a caterpillar doing the worm when they moved—"you help me refill the jar."

Wait. Fort started to shake his head. "I don't think—"

"That's a *wonderful* idea," Mama said. "Fortitude, you go on and help Mr. G. I gotta get back inside and help out. Go on, now! Aunt Netta wouldn't have wanted you 'round outside anyway."

Mama's tone left no room for argument, and—if he was being honest—she was right. Aunt Netta always told him moping and a quarter could buy him a soda.

The world is harsh. Find your joy, Fortitude, and it'll be your night-light when everything is dark.

So, before Mama's eyes could narrow, he dusted off his pants and stood. "Yes, Mama."

She nodded, kissed his forehead, and went inside. It was hard on her, being not quite nine months pregnant and losing one of her closest friends in Aunt Netta. Fort tried to help out, tried to do as much as he could for her, but getting in trouble was definitely *not* making things easier.

"Well then, young Fortitude."

Fort turned to find Mr. G studying him, before the man handed him a butterfly net, two nickels, and a broken bubble wand. Fort held all the items, confused, but the old man had already twirled around (yes, twirled, with more agility than seemed possible) and pranced over (yes, pranced, is this going to be a thing?) to the wagon before Fort could ask any questions—like what, exactly, they were meant to be collecting. Mr. G tucked the jar inside, then pulled out a bright blue nylon roll. He yanked a cord, skipped backward, then clapped his hands together and laughed.

Fort stared in amazement. Where there had been nothing but painted yellow lines in the church parking lot there now stood a large inflatable door.

A *door.*

Fort rubbed his eyes, blinked, then squinted.

Mr. G was already lugging the wagon and whistling as he unzipped the air-filled entrance and pulled it open. Instead of revealing the other side of the parking lot, bright and sweltering in the midday sun, Fort saw cool darkness and silver stars dangling at ground level on the other side.

"Come on, young man, come on! The final delivery of joy must be collected if balance is to be found!" And the strange old man danced through the doorway, the wagon disappearing behind him.

Fort stepped closer to the door. It shimmered as he approached, and . . . was it growing bigger? He could smell something delicious coming from inside . . . like . . . apple turnovers. Fort looked back at the church. He couldn't go back there—if Mama didn't catch him, someone else would and he'd still get in trouble. It takes a village to ground a child, apparently.

"Well?"

Fort startled out of his thoughts.

Mr. G stuck his head out the doorway and frowned. "Aren't you coming to help?"

Find your joy, Fortitude.

Fort took a deep breath, nodded, and stepped into wonder.

Imagine walking through the stars. An interactive planetarium where you can reach out and touch worlds. Galaxies. Nebulas. Clusters of suns that appear and disappear with every step. Imagine trailing your fingers through the tail of a comet that burns through space right beside you. Fort saw all this and more.

Mama would flip if she was here. Did she know about it? She always did love to look at the stars, point out meteors, and just sit and hum under the light of the moon. As Fort turned in wonder, a planet the size of a beach ball with two marble-sized moons floated toward him.

"What is this place?" he whispered.

"The Between." Mr. G's voice came from somewhere ahead. "The realm between worlds."

"A different realm?"

"And a shortcut." The old man appeared to Fort's left. As he pulled his wagon, he was sprinkling what looked like sparks into the air above his head. When he reached Fort he stopped, turned around, and blew out a strong puff of air. The sparks scattered, speckling the dark and twinkling.

They're stars, Fort realized.

Mr. G dusted his hands and nodded thoughtfully. "Traveling from world to world would be terribly inefficient if not for the Between. Could you imagine the fuel costs? Astronomical. Not to mention all the rest stops. No, no, simply impossible. But we have the Between, and thus the joy can be collected like that!" He snapped a finger. "Now, where's that net?"

"What do you mean, joy?" Fort asked as he handed over the butterfly net. "How did you find this place?"

Mr. G laughed. "Find? Ha! No one finds the Between, young one. They are shown. Led. Taught. My teacher showed me, and now I show you. This will be your responsibility soon."

"Me? Why?"

The old man reached forward, his hand disappearing behind Fort's head, then reappearing with one of the nickels he'd given the boy. "Balance. You wondered why there had to be so much sadness, my boy. Oh, don't make that face, I know you were thinking it. And where there's a question, there must be an answer. Besides, you broke the collecting jar, so now you have to replenish the joy. Your mother said so."

The words whizzed around Fort's head like moons around a planet. Nothing made sense. Maybe he could sneak back and find the weird inflatable door, and then he could go back to . . .

To what? To Aunt Netta's homegoing? To be alone with the sadness again? *No.* He might as well help the strange old man. Maybe if he spent enough time here, the pain he felt would go away.

Besides, the Between was pretty cool.

"Okay," Fort said, taking a deep breath. "So we have to collect joy, whatever that means. How can I help?"

Mr. G grinned, held out a tiny bottle labeled *Gary the Griot's Splendiferous Story Solution* and the bubble wand (now taped back together), then brandished the butterfly net like a baseball bat. "Looks like there's a story of joy ready to be told."

He nodded at the planet that bobbed waist-high next to Fort. "Blow the bubbles at that world, my young Fortitude."

"But . . ." Fort hesitated. "Why bubbles?"

"Joy is a fragile thing, my boy, and must be treated as such. Too harsh and it disintegrates. Rush, and it disappears. So we coax it forth. Feed it, like kindling to a fire."

"So . . . you're saying we should do something fun in order to draw it out?"

Mr. G snapped his fingers and pointed. "That's it! And what's more fun than blowing bubbles? Nothing. Unless you're blowing one of my patented splendiferous bubbles."

O . . . kaaaay.

Fort opened his mouth, then closed it and shook his head. Whatever. He turned, dipped the wand into the jar, then pulled it out and blew a gentle stream of air through the circles at the planet. Rainbow-colored bubbles collided with the tiny clouds. Dozens. Hundreds. Soon the planet was covered and the bubbles began to multiply. They combined, split, then joined again, forming one giant bubble that engulfed the world, and on its surface . . .

"I see something!" Fort shouted.

"Excellent!" Mr. G said. "What do you see?"

Fort leaned in. "Well, there's a boy with a list . . ."

Mr. G deftly snagged the giant bubble, now heavy with shimmering, smaller bubbles inside. Fort saw faces, grins, celebrations dance across their surface.

"Is that joy?" he asked.

The bubble wobbled into the giant jar, where it promptly burst. Fort placed a hand on the jar, then jerked back. The glass felt warm. And there was a pulsing, rhythmic hum running along it—as if something, or someone, was singing.

Mr. G leaned on the net and wiped his brow. "Requires a lot of concentration, making the transfer. Not as young as I was a hundred years ago. Now, what did you ask? Joy? Yes! That's the joy. But no time to dawdle, young Fortitude. We've more worlds to visit, more joy to find! Forthwith!"

THERE'S GOING TO BE A FIGHT IN THE CAFETERIA ON FRIDAY AND YOU BETTER NOT BRING BATMAN

BY LAMAR GILES

Batman (perma-banned)

~~Spider-Man~~

~~Captain America~~

~~Superman~~

~~War Machine~~

~~Wonder Woman~~

~~Thor~~

~~Iron Man~~

~~The Hulk~~

~~The Winter Soldier~~

~~The Flash~~

~~Wolverine~~

~~Doctor Strange~~

~~Thanos~~

~~Black Panther~~

The school bus squealed to a stop at the corner by Cornell's house. Other kids from the neighborhood got off, but he was too busy rereading that stupid list to notice. Black Panther gone. Superman gone. The Hulk—

"Cornell!" Mr. Jeffries shouted from the driver's

seat. "You ain't about to have me doubling back because you missed your stop again. Pay attention!"

"Sorry. Sorry." Cornell scooted from his seat and brushed past his laughing schoolmates, including Amaya Arnold. Amaya was more *giggling* than *laughing*, and Cornell could tell she wasn't being mean. Actually, her giggle was kind of pretty. Almost as pretty as her.

But he wasn't brave enough to look her way too long, so his eyes wandered . . . to Tobin Pitts. Who was staring at him. Hard.

Tobin swiped his red bangs away from his eyes and freckled forehead. "Hope you're ready."

Cornell shook his head and exited the bus with that stupid list taking up the space in his head he'd rather reserve for Amaya.

But, unless she got superpowers before lunch tomorrow, she wasn't going to be much help.

The cars in the driveway told Cornell everyone was home except Mom, who was still on the West Coast for her business trip. He weaved between Carter's beat-up burgundy Chevy "starter car," Dad's might-be-time-for-an-upgrade-if-he-can-convince-Mom black Audi, and Pop-Pop's classics-are-the-way-to-go baby blue Cadillac until he reached the side door. He removed the lanyard from his neck where his single silver key dangled and jiggled it in the knob.

Before she left, Mom had told them all, "Don't think because I'm away it's supposed to be Bruhs Gone Wild. I want this house looking like humans live here when I get back."

Inside, the funky-ripe smell of the overfull kitchen trash can suggested they had work to do.

First things first, though. "Carter! Hey, Carter! I need your help."

Cornell's brother wasn't in the kitchen, and the house wasn't shaking from rap bass, so he probably wasn't in his bedroom. Cornell rushed through the dining room, scooted by Mom's home office, cut through the foyer, kicked his shoes off before stepping into the living room no one ever sat in, and came to a skidding stop at the den, where he found his brother on the wraparound couch with a guest.

"Hi," Cornell said, surprised.

The girl gushed. "Oh, you must be Carter's brother!"

She had dark brown skin, supercool red-framed glasses, and an Afro puff on each side of her head. She reminded Cornell of Amaya. Her jean jacket had a bunch of buttons pinned to the collar and pockets. Cornell leaned forward, trying to read some—BLACK LIVES

MATTER; LOVE IS LOVE—when Carter reminded them he was in the room. "Whatchu need, Lil' Man?"

Cornell's chin jerked up. Carter never called him "Lil' Man" before. Also, "Why's your voice sound like that?"

Carter coughed and cleared his throat. The weird deepness became his normal little-bit-whiny voice. "We're studying."

The girl told Carter, "Hey, I want *you* to introduce *me* to this little cutie."

Cornell smiled. "Thank you!"

Mom taught him how to take a compliment.

Carter . . . was not smiling. "Raven, that's Cornell. Cornell, Raven. What. Do. You. Want?"

"Oh, right!" Cornell fished the list from his back pocket and hopped over the back of the couch. It was a nimble leap. He landed right between the study buddies.

Raven clapped like Cornell had done some YouTube-level parkour. Carter stared, his face twitching in a super weird way. He was probably just focusing real hard so he could be as helpful as possible, Cornell figured.

"There's this thing that happens in the cafeteria on Fridays," Cornell said, "where everyone gathers around and argues about which superheroes can do what. Sometimes it's just about who's better, and sometimes it's about who would beat who in a fight. It's a big thing. Anyway, my name got pulled out the hat again, so I have

20

to go tomorrow, except I can't use any of the characters on this list because—"

Carter stood up.

Oh.

Maybe he thought better on his feet.

"Come with me." Carter left the room.

Cornell hopped off the couch and waved bye to Raven.

He found Carter in the kitchen, leaning on the fridge, his face tight. "Do you see what's happening out there?"

"Yeah, you're studying with Raven."

Carter's chest heaved. He snatched the paper from Cornell's hand. "Gimme that list."

"Rude."

His eyebrows rose. "Batman's perma-banned?"

"Yep. Everyone thinks he's overrated. Plus, it's not cool how he practices his karate on, like, his neighbors."

"True. Don't even get me started on him fighting Superman. I mean, an orbital blast of Heat Vision beats a stupid bat-shaped boomerang any day of the week."

"That's what I said."

Carter's mouth screwed up. He rubbed the back of his head with one hand. "You need a super who's not on this list?"

"No!" Cornell got to the really alarming part he was trying to explain on the couch. "I need *three*. Tomorrow's category is Battle Royale *Trios*."

"Y'all have categories? That is weirdly precise." He seemed impressed.

"It's the last debate before school's out and I always lose. Help. Me."

"Okay, okay." Carter cracked the fridge, grabbed three ginger ales in the glass bottles that Dad liked while he contemplated the list.

Cornell plucked the magnetized bottle opener from the fridge door and popped the caps off. He liked the clinking noise they made when they hit the granite counter.

"Can't use Black Panther?" Carter said.

"Naw."

"Luke Cage?"

Cornell pointed to the back of the sheet. Luke Cage had already been used in a previous battle, too.

"Black Green Lantern?"

Cornell chewed his lip. "Someone used a white Green Lantern before, so since they're both Green Lantern, it might not work."

"That's trash," Carter said, but moved on. "You really gotta know your stuff to work these rules. Okay, seems to me you need a pretty versatile team to be safe. Someone techy. Someone magic. Maybe some kind of wild card. Like a telepath, or a *teleporter*."

"If Shuri or Riri Williams isn't on the list, you've still got good techy options." Raven stood in the doorway between the kitchen and the den, obviously catching all of their conversation even though they'd tried to be quiet.

Carter straightened, then sort of leaned diagonal on the counter like someone was about to take his picture. "Bae, didn't know you were into this."

He was also back to his funky not-normal voice. What was wrong with him?

Raven joined them at the counter. "May I see your list, Cornell?"

"Yep." He passed it to her.

Raven smoothed the paper on the countertop, reviewed it, then flipped it over. "Can I have a pen, please?"

Cornell looked to Carter. Carter looked confused but retrieved a pen from the junk drawer. Raven began quick scribbling on the list. Then: "Here."

Batman (perma- banned)	~~Thor~~	~~Doctor Strange~~
~~Spider-Man~~ Silk	~~Iron Man~~ Riri/ Ironheart	~~Thanos~~
~~Captain America~~	~~The Hulk~~ She-Hulk	~~Black Panther~~ Shuri
~~Superman~~	~~The Winter Soldier~~	
~~War Machine~~		
~~Wonder Woman~~ Nubia	~~The Flash~~	
	~~Wolverine~~ X-23	

23

Cornell didn't know what to say. This was genius.

"Pro tip," Raven said, "don't sleep on the ladies. Now you have options."

Carter gawked like he'd just met a real-life superhero. "Who are you?"

"Fan Girl," Raven said. "Now we probably should do a little studying."

"Absolutely." Carter grabbed two ginger ales and led Raven away.

Cornell went over the list again; Raven poked her head back in the room.

She said, "I don't know the rules for your debates, but in case your friends say you can't swap She-Hulk for Hulk or something, you might want some backups."

She was right. Of course. "Thanks, Raven. I'm glad you can tolerate Carter enough to be here."

Carter yelled, "Go. Away!"

But Cornell was already gone. Darting to the rec room for Dad's advice.

Hopefully he was as good as Raven.

○ ○ ○

"*. . . All right, you Workout Warriors! Keep the High-Intensity Interval Training blast-off going! Twenty-eight, twenty-nine, thirty . . .*"

One of the really energetic but a little bit scary train-ers from Dad's workout app screamed instructions Cor-nell heard before he entered the rec room. He burst in, found Dad on the couch sweaty and gasping.

Dad spotted Cornell and leapt up, rejoining the workout streaming on their big TV with an out-of-sync burpee.

"Thirty-two," he said, "thirty-three, thirty . . . hey, son. Let me pause this real quick."

Dad's hand shook when he exited out of the work-out video instead of pausing it, then closed the app al-together.

"Whew! Good workout." He heavy-gasped three times, then dropped to one knee like he needed to tie his shoe even though both sneakers were double-knotted. "Never stop moving, son. Never. Stop. Moving."

Cornell was concerned about his father's hard breath-ing. "Do you want to lie back on the couch, Dad?"

"After . . . *that*? No way. That was light work." He squeezed one eye shut against the sweat pouring off his forehead. "You need something?"

Dad looked like Carter (*and, I guess, me,* Cornell thought) just wider, with less hair on his head, but more (*gray!*) hair on his face. He liked cool bands like the Roots and really good singers like Mary J. Blige, and insisted they were better than Carter's and Cornell's music—sometimes, maybe, they were. Dad loved funny Eddie Murphy movies, and serious TV like CNN and *Divorce Court,* and often wanted the whole family in the rec room on Saturday nights to play Monopoly or UNO. Since the superhero battles were kind of like a game, he might be into it. Cornell showed him the updated list and explained what he was looking for.

"I see," Dad said. "Does it have to be strictly comics?"

"Naw. Someone said John Wick once and everyone was okay with it. Then the John Wick kid tried to say John Wick could use Kryptonite bullets. We all knew that was wrong, though."

"Uh-huh." Dad was still gasping, but less.

"Raven, Carter's friend, gave me a good techy option with Riri Williams. Carter said it might not hurt to have a magic user."

Dad perked. "That's easy, then. Kazaam's your guy."

"Shazam?" Cornell flipped the list, almost certain that hero had been used, too.

Dad said, "Not *SHA*-zam. *KA*-zaam. The genie basketball legend Shaquille O'Neal played in the best movie of 1996."

"Uhhhhhh."

"Let me show you." Dad opened the movie app on the TV and scrolled through the family library to the Ks.

"We *own Kazaam*?"

"Boy, I've owned *Kazaam* on VHS, DVD, Blu-ray—had to buy that one international because apparently the United States dropped the ball there—and now on digital."

"Why?" The thumbnail photo of the basketball giant in golden genie clothes and the floppy-haired kid star of the film looked ridiculous.

Dad's breathing was normal again—thank goodness—and he shambled to the couch, patting the cushion next to him. Cornell took a seat.

"This movie came out when I was about your brother's age. To be honest, I got excited whenever I saw Black guys like us on the big screen. Pop-Pop would take me and your grandma to see any movie that Black folks were a part of, and I loved them all, even if they sometimes seemed silly."

Dad worked the remote, scrolling through other movies in their digital library that Cornell never noticed. "There's *The Meteor Man. Blankman. Steel*—another Shaq classic. *Spawn. Blade.* Those last two we might watch when you're a little older. If you want, I mean."

"How come you never showed me these before?" They watched movies together all the time, but never these.

"I tried with Carter when you were very young, but he

wasn't into it. Your generation have a lot of different—and better—things than me and your mom had. I get it. I still keep all this because I love it, and . . ." He wrung his hands in a way that made Cornell feel a little sad. "I like having something for y'all from when I was young. Even if you don't need it."

Cornell took his list back, pressed it onto his thigh so he could write. He scribbled down his new additions.

Batman (perma-banned)	~~Thor~~	~~Doctor Strange~~
~~Spider-Man~~ Silk	~~Iron Man~~ Riri/ Ironheart	~~Thanos~~
~~Captain America~~	~~The Hulk~~ She-Hulk	~~Black Panther~~ Shuri
~~Superman~~	~~The Winter Soldier~~	kazaam???
~~War Machine~~		Meteor Man
~~Wonder Woman~~ Nubia	~~The Flash~~	Blankman
	~~Wolverine~~ X-23	

Cornell hopped off the couch. "Dad, I don't know about those Shaquille O'Neal movies, but could we maybe watch *Meteor Man* this weekend? His costume's cool."

Dad beamed! And looked way less like he needed to go to the hospital. "Of course. Just catch me after

I'm done working out Saturday. Gotta keep my six-pack tight." He rubbed his round belly and cackled.

"Love you, Dad," Cornell said on his way out.

"Love you too."

"Hey, you said Pop-Pop took you to see those movies?"

"Every last one."

Cornell jogged up the stairs, bypassing his bedroom for the one at the far end of the hall. Pop-Pop's.

Time they had a little chat about his taste in film.

Cornell knocked, a three-part rhythm. *Ta-da-thump!*

Pop-Pop called from the other side, "Who dat?"

Pop-Pop knew full well who it was because that *Ta-da-thump* was *Cornell's knock,* but this was part of the game they'd played since he was little-little. "It's Cornell Curry, your grandson, Pop-Pop."

"Are you sure you're Cornell and not some sneak thief coming for my gold?"

"The only gold you have is your tooth."

"Well, I definitely ain't letting you in, then. Because if you a sneak thief, how I'm supposed to chew?"

It was silly, and didn't make a lot of sense, but they'd been doing it since Cornell was four years old, and it still felt a little funny. Cornell knew it wasn't something they'd do forever. But it was fine for now, and that was okay.

Cornell turned the knob, stepped inside, and immediately began coughing. His eyes burned. What was happening?

"Close that there door for me, Nelly."

Cornell cupped his hand over his nose and mouth. "Are you sure?"

"Yep. Need your opinion on something."

Sealing them in, Cornell adjusted to the weird scent his brain identified as spicy lemon juice ocean water.

Pop-Pop said, "I got Bible study tonight and Miss Felicia down at the church sent me one of them text messagings with a winky face saying she liked the cologne I had on the other Sunday. Thing is I switch it up *every* Sunday because you got to be unpredictable." He motioned to a silver tray on his dresser that was jam-packed with half-drained cologne bottles. "Remember that, Cornell. Never let 'em see you comin'!"

"Who?"

"So Miss Felicia missed a couple of Sundays 'cause she was visiting her grandkids down in Florida. And I'm so unpredictable, I done went and fooled myself. I don't remember exactly which one I was wearing last time I saw her."

Pop-Pop held two fancy colognes for Cornell to see.

One in murky blue glass shaped like a seashell. The other in a smoke gray bottle that looked like a test tube. Pop-Pop spritzed both nozzles at the same time and Cornell flinched away like bugs do when you shoot them with bug spray.

"Which one you like best?"

Cornell gagged. "Neither."

"Boy! This ain't no time to be joking around."

"I just started wearing deodorant last month, Pop-Pop."

Pop-Pop narrowed his eyes, nodding. "I s'pose you have a point. You don't know what you don't know. I'mma get you started with a Tommy Bahama gift set from down at the CVS for your birthday, though. Every man needs a supply of Smell Goods. You hear me?"

"I hear you, Pop-Pop. Can I ask you about something?"

"Always."

"Okay . . ." Cornell recapped what he was facing in his superhero fight tomorrow, what he and Carter discussed, and how the discussion with Raven—who was very smart and pretty, the more Cornell thought about it—was better than the discussion with Carter, then what he and Dad discussed about Pop-Pop taking him and Grandma to see movies about Black heroes when Dad was a kid. Cornell finished with, "I wanna know who you think the best heroes are."

"Well," Pop-Pop said, leaning back in his chair, really thinking it over, "the ultimate superhero is the Lord."

Cornell blinked.

Pop-Pop scratched at his beard. "S'pose that wouldn't be a fair fight, now would it? Hmmm. Explain this here debate to me again."

"I've got two potential picks—one from Raven, one from Dad. I need a third."

"I've always been partial to John Shaft."

"Never heard of him."

"He's a complicated man. No one understands him like his woman!"

The way Pop-Pop said it, Cornell figured it was supposed to mean something more than what it sounded like. Maybe?

Pop-Pop huffed. "You kids today, I swear. That line is from Shaft's theme song. The man had his own song, Nelly."

"That sounds cool."

"It was. Coolest thing ever. Look. When I was growing up you didn't see a lot of us in the pictures. Then, in the 1970s, Black filmmakers decided enough of that, we gon' be the stars of our own movies, and they made a bunch where we were detectives, and kung fu masters, and even vampires!"

"Vampires?" That sounded even cooler.

"Now, some of them movies were better than others, but people who name stuff named them all 'blaxploitation' films. And, for my money, Shaft was king of the blaxploitation bunch. Way better than them Captain Spider-Hulks y'all mess with. Such a shame you never really got to know your grandma. On our first date she picked the movie. *Shaft in Africa*."

Cornell perked. "He's a king from Africa? Like Black Panther?"

"We all are!"

Cornell got his list out, added to it.

Batman (perma-banned)	~~Thor~~	~~Doctor Strange~~
~~Spider-Man~~ Silk	~~Iron Man~~ Riri/ Ironheart	~~Thanos~~
~~Captain America~~	~~The Hulk~~ She-Hulk	~~Black Panther~~ Shuri
~~Superman~~	~~The Winter Soldier~~	Kazaam???
~~War Machine~~	~~The Flash~~	Meteor Man
~~Wonder Woman~~ Nubia	~~Wolverine~~ X-23	Blankman
		John Shaft

Pop-Pop said, "Back in the day, the best cologne was a brand known as Hai Karate. I bet that's what John Shaft wore. They stopped making it about forty years ago, but I've saved the last little bit I had for a special occasion."

He rummaged through his dozens of cologne bottles and retrieved one that was green and glowing like the plutonium stick on *The Simpsons*. "Wanna smell it?"

Cornell had already flung Pop-Pop's door open and was halfway down the hall. "Maybe later. Gotta put my team together."

A daring escape. Made in just the nick of time.

That evening, when Mom called for family FaceTime, Raven had gone home, Dad had showered, and Pop-Pop had just a few minutes before he had to leave for Bible study. All four of the Curry men gathered around Dad's iPad for a view of Mom's face as it filled the screen.

"All my fellas. Hey there!" she said.

They sounded off. All glad to see her. Cornell hadn't talked to the others much about it, but he missed her a bunch when she went out of town.

"How's the shoot going?" Dad asked.

"Fantastic," Mom said. "Might be the best adaptation of my work yet."

Mom's job was writing mystery books. So far, Hollywood had made three movies based on them. She was visiting the set of the fourth. She asked, "What have y'all been up to?"

Everyone told a messy, pieced together version of helping Cornell with his superhero team.

Mom nodded through the explanation. "Okay. Cornell, have you settled on your heroes?"

The truth was he'd wanted to ask Mom first. She had the best imagination in the house, knew all kinds of stuff about comics, books, movies, songs, history, science . . . everything. Dad always said Cornell and Carter were lucky because they got half their genes from a genius, and the other half from him. Cornell hadn't wanted to bother her on her movie set, though.

But since she'd asked . . .

"I'm close," Cornell said. "Do you have any ideas?"

"Sort of. Why don't you make up your own heroes?"

"I—" The thought stunned him. "I think that's against the rules."

"I used to think that too, sweetie. Then I did it anyway."

Someone on Mom's side of the call yelled, "Janice, you got a moment? Mr. Peele wants to discuss some script changes with you."

Mom spoke over her shoulder. "Be right there." Then, to her fellas, she said, "I gotta run. I'll call back if it's not too late. Love y'all."

"We love you too," they said together like they'd rehearsed. Dad's iPad reverted to the Washington Wizards home screen and the call crowd dispersed.

Carter got a text from Raven and ran upstairs goofy-grinning. Dad heard the guest bathroom toilet running and went to investigate because he might have to hit Home Depot. Pop-Pop rolled out because he didn't want to keep Miss Felicia waiting.

Cornell remained alone at the counter with his list. Thinking. About what he might do anyway.

The next day Cornell boarded his bus, ignoring Tobin's taunting "I hope you're ready."

Cornell felt good about it. He had his team picked, plus some extras.

Amaya, with her hair in ribbons, smiled when he passed. He took the seat behind her and said, "Hey."

She twisted so they were eye to eye, looking somewhat surprised. "Hey."

"I wanna show you something." Cornell unfolded a sheet of paper for her to see. Not the list—he was kinda over that—but a drawing. He was a decent artist, and after talking to Mom, he thought about what a cool hero of his own design might look like.

Amaya gawked, then snatched the paper. "Oh my goodness."

It was a hero named Fan Girl, who wore Amaya's favorite color—red, Cornell had noticed—and had her same long hair, with a matching mask and cape.

"She looks like me," Amaya said, amazed.

Cornell grinned the grin he'd seen Carter practicing, laughed like his father, trusted that the single spritz of Pop-Pop's cologne (not Hai Karate) was just enough, and let her in on the secret his mom told him. "Apparently, that's a thing we can do. I thought you should know!"

As the bus pulled away from the curb, Cornell Curry felt like a winner. And the day was only going to get better.

THE McCOY GAME

BY B. B. ALSTON

Ma steers the truck off the dirt road, parking in a grassy field. She takes a hard look at Uncle Ray's cherry red Corvette up ahead and rolls her eyes. "This must be the place."

I press my face to the passenger-side window and frown. All these years, and Big Mac never said anything about having a whole extra house in the middle of nowhere. If you can even call it a house—it's more like a small mansion. Type of place where fancy people live.

Which didn't exactly describe my grandad.

But I'm not *that* surprised. Nobody in the family was, not really. Old dude loved his secrets. Almost as much as he loved calling me "youngin" whenever the family got together.

Ma just shakes her head. "I don't care what your grandaddy said in that letter, Jamal, I don't like the idea of you going in there alone."

I shrug. "Dre will be there too."

"You mean the cousin who was your best friend in the world and now y'all act like strangers? That Dre?"

I blow out a sigh. "Ma, it's complicated." I'm tempted to remind her that she and Dre's dad, my uncle Ray, don't get along either, but last time I did that Ma went on and on about how I need to stay out of grown folks' business.

"You'd rather let Dre and Uncle Ray have the house?" I say instead. "They don't even need another place. Just don't want us getting it."

She frowns at that. Didn't think so.

"Well, I'm gonna head inside," I say quickly.

Ma just nods. "I'll be right here. Call if you need me."

The midsummer heat swallows me up as soon as I leave the truck. Even in the shade of the few trees between the road and the house, the heated breeze is like a blow-dryer pointed directly in my face. By the time I jog up to the front door, I'm already sweating.

The door swings open before I can knock.

"Took you long enough." Dre towers over me in the doorway. He's the tallest kid at our middle school, taller even than Uncle Ray, who used to hoop professionally overseas. If today were any other Saturday, Dre would be playing in some AAU tournament—competing against the best high school ballers in the state. He's that good.

But Big Mac's funeral was a few weeks back. And

Dre got handed the same black envelope that I did. There was a letter inside:

Jamal—

Look at all these people carrying on like I'm really dead. They must not know our secret, huh? McCoys don't die!

Hope you still remember what I taught you about reading coordinates because I got a surprise for ya! You and your cousin should come and see for yourself. ALONE!

I'm putting the key to all my secrets in y'all's hands.

—Big Mac

The coordinates were written on the back. Folks laughed when we showed them the letters Grandad sent. Typical Big Mac always playing his pranks, they said. Even Ma shook her head and grinned. "That's my daddy, always got to have the last laugh."

That laughter got quiet after I tracked the coordinates to an old house way out in the country listed under Grandad's government name: Gerald McCoy. And then things really got interesting the following week when the guy reading the will said the property could only be inherited by one of his grandkids, and only if all of the requirements are fulfilled.

One of his grandkids.

But while everybody else is worried about how much the house might be worth, I've been thinking about what Big Mac said in that letter. *McCoys don't die . . .* Which, I know, sounds impossible, but if you ever spent a summer with Big Mac, you'd know "impossible" wasn't a word he believed in. I can't help wondering if the house isn't the real surprise—maybe he's still alive somehow.

"You going to let me in or what?" I say, pushing past Dre into the small entryway of the house. Two more large wooden doors block the rest of the way. I reach for the knobs.

"Already tried it," says Dre. "Locked."

"Well, there's got to be some way in." I scan the space until I find a small sign that reads KEYS above an empty key rack. Just below it sits a pile of rusted metal parts.

I'm about to turn back to the door when I notice a button on one of the metal pieces. I lean in closer. Big Mac always said, "You're either a doer, or a spectator. And the world already got enough spectators." So I reach out and press the button. I mean, what's the worst that could—

The stack of metal moves and I stumble backward into Dre.

"Ay! Watch where you going," he grumbles and

shoves me away. We glare at each other until a loud whirring sound gets our attention. Those rusted pieces begin to shift and spin until they've rearranged themselves into a short robot with glowing silver eyes. "KEY DROID OPERATIONAL . . ."

I glance back at Dre, slack-jawed. He shrugs.

"I ASSUME YOU TWO ARE JAMAL AND ANDRE?" the robot squeaks.

"Y-Yeah, that's us," Dre stutters. "The heck you supposed to be?"

The robot rolls its silver eyes. "HAVE YOU REALLY NEVER SEEN A KEY DROID BEFORE?"

"Um, I'm gonna say nah . . . ," I reply.

"WELL, IT'S REALLY SELF-EXPLANATORY, ISN'T IT? A KEY DROID OPENS DOORS . . . I DARESAY IF YOU FIND ME CONFUSING, YOU'RE IN FOR QUITE A SHOCK . . ."

Dre and I just stare at the thing. Are we really talking to an actual robot right now?

"OH BOY. I'M IN FOR A LONG AFTERNOON, AREN'T I?" The key droid waddles past us to the locked door and extends a finger that also happens to be a small key. The droid pushes it into the lock and two clicks later the large door creaks open.

The great room beyond is huge, like *huge* huge. The polished hardwood floors shine even in the dim light, and tall, very old-looking paintings hang from the walls.

Rising from the center of the room are twin staircases that bend away from each other and meet on a higher floor, overlooking where we're standing.

But nice as all that might be, it's not what holds my attention. The ceiling overhead is covered in twinkling white shimmers, like a starry night sky. A great big fireball burns ferociously in midair while golden spheres zip around orbits and burning meteors streak across the room. It's *incredible*. . . .

"It's a model of the solar system," says Dre. "Those gold orbs are the planets, and see that cloud of dust floating between Mars and Jupiter? I bet that's supposed to be the asteroid belt . . ."

"AH, SO YOU DO KNOW SOMETHING!" the key droid exclaims. "I REALLY WAS BEGINNING TO QUESTION THE OLD MAN'S JUDGMENT. HONESTLY, TO NOT EVEN KNOW WHAT A KEY DROID IS . . ."

"Man, Big Mac loved *anything* to do with outer space," I say. He taught Dre and me to care about it too. Each summer we'd spend at his trailer, he'd take us outside whenever the night was clear and we'd stare up at the stars. And then he'd tell us stories about all the crazy made-up space missions he'd had when he was younger. Those tales were wild enough to be a Netflix series.

"Old dude had to be sitting on some serious cash for a room like this," says Dre.

"See, I knew that's all you cared about. *You* didn't even spend last summer with Grandad. Shouldn't even be here."

"Yeah, whatever," says Dre. "You just worry about yourself." He turns to the droid. "So how we doing this? Deciding who gets the house, I mean."

"IT'S SIMPLE," the key droid explains, pointing to the opposite side of the room. "WHOEVER PASSES THROUGH THAT GOLDEN DOOR INHERITS THE HOUSE."

Dre and I both take a long look at the golden door at the back of the great room—and the oversized keyhole at its center.

"Is Grandad behind that door?" I promise I didn't mean to say that out loud.

Dre bursts out laughing. "You really dumb as you look, aren't you? What you think the funeral was for? The old man is gone."

I ball my fists. "Call me dumb again!"

"Or what?" Dre taunts.

"SAVE YOUR ENERGY!" shouts the key droid, shutting us both up. "NOW THEN, SHOULD WE HAVE A LOOK AT THE GOLDEN DOOR OR WOULD YOU RATHER COMPETE FOR A KEY?"

"That key is about to be mine," says Dre. "Lead the way, metal dude."

"Yeah, let's get this over with. We both know *I'm* winning that key."

Dre and I follow the key droid across the great room, shooting each other angry looks the whole way. We end up in a bright hallway, tall glass display cases lining the walls. Inside, great hunks of stone, some smooth, others jagged like cave walls, are covered in ancient-looking drawings of brown-skinned men and women floating in the sky and the heavens above.

See, Big Mac had this theory that there are these really cool caretakers that look out for all life in the universe. Humanity was born in Africa, and Grandad said those caretakers stopped by early on to teach us stuff like math and science. Basically how to survive and thrive. Said they even took some of us up on their ships to see the galaxy. It always sounded like a science fiction book to me, but looking at these drawings . . . I don't know what to think anymore.

The hallway ends at another locked door. The key droid unlocks it and we step into a vast library, great columns of shelved books reaching up to the second-story ceiling. I have to tilt my head back to see that high.

"OVER HERE," calls the key droid. It points to two glass helmets and two shiny metal backpacks hanging on the wall just beside the door.

45

"What do we do with these?"

The key droid throws up its hands. "CLEARLY THE HELMETS GO OVER YOUR HEAD, AND THE BACKPACKS GO ON YOUR BACK."

"Oh, um, yeah, that makes sense." I scratch my chin. "But why—"

"JUST PUT THEM ON, WILL YOU?"

"Fine, fine. Don't have to be rude." I slip the helmet over my head and strap on the backpack. They're much lighter than they look.

"NOW, IF YOU'LL BOTH LISTEN VERY CLOSELY, THE RULES ARE SIMPLE. SEE THAT KEY UP THERE?" The key droid points its stubby little arm toward a glinting piece of metal high up on one of the columns. "THAT'S WHAT YOU'RE AFTER."

"How are we supposed to reach that?" asks Dre. "I might be able to dunk, but I can't jump that high."

A cackle escapes the key droid. "THEN WHY DON'T I ADJUST THE GRAVITY?" It reaches back to turn a dial on the wall and my whole body feels instantly lighter. Dre takes a step backward and ends up gliding like ten feet.

"ACT FAST! YOU ONLY HAVE TWO MINUTES!" With that, the key droid turns the dial as far as it will go, and I feel my feet leave the ground completely as I float up toward the ceiling. I wave my arms to steady myself, but that just makes it worse. And there's nothing close enough to hold on to up here.

That's when I see Dre speed past me, a stream of smoke pouring out of his backpack.

Wait, this backpack is actually a jet pack? I pat it down, looking for a power button, and manage to locate a tiny on switch. Here goes nothing . . .

I flip it and zip forward, becoming lost in the cloud of books that have all floated up from the shelves. It takes me a moment to get the hang of this thing, but then it clicks that I have to lean my head and shoulders in the direction I want to go. It's a lot like swimming in midair.

I guide myself over to where we saw the key, only it's not there. For a second, I think I've already lost, that Dre must've gotten to it before I could. But then I catch sight of him flying in a wide arcing circle below me, hands empty, his head whipping back and forth in search of the key.

The key must've floated away from its shelf too. And now it's lost somewhere in all these books. I glance around frantically, heart pounding as I feel the two-minute time limit slipping away.

And then I see the key. Bouncing along the ceiling.

I angle myself so that the jet pack lifts me higher, book after book clanging against my glass helmet. I can't help but grin as the key finally comes into reach, and I extend an arm to grab it. It's so close now, I can reach out and touch—

Something slams into me and I go tumbling backward, head over heels. So fast, I don't know what's up and what's down. I'm totally out of control!

"TIME'S UP!"

The jet pack jolts me to a sudden stop. The library spins before my eyes. I blink the dizziness away until Dre's smirking face comes into focus. At least he doesn't have the key.

"Too slow, cuz!" He laughs.

"That key was mine!" As the jet pack lowers me gently to the floor, I'm so mad I could shout. "You cheated!"

Dre just shrugs. "Nobody said we couldn't play rough. Get your weight up."

The key droid waddles between us. "IT APPEARS NEITHER OF YOU OBTAINED THE KEY."

"You happy now?" I ask Dre. "We lost our only chance at the key."

"As long as you didn't get it," he says sourly.

"WELL, THERE IS ONE MORE KEY. A SECOND CHANCE, AS THEY SAY. BUT I WARN YOU IT'S NOT WITHOUT RISK. FAR MORE DANGEROUS THAN A FEW FLOATING BOOKS."

"Dangerous?" Dre suddenly looks sick. "How dangerous?"

"GIANT BREATHWORM DANGEROUS."

"The heck is a breathworm?" asks Dre.

I grin and cross my arms. "Nah, Dre, you don't care about space stuff anymore, remember?" That's what he said when I got back from space camp and he decided to stop hanging out with me. And Grandad, too. All of a sudden his life was all about basketball—he was too cool for us.

He and I have spoken more today than we have in the past year.

"What does space got to do with a breathworm?"

"That's where they live," I say. "Big Mac told me about them last summer."

Dre's fear melts away and he starts laughing. "Oh, so it's just one of Grandad's space monsters from those silly stories? Man, let's do this."

The key droid takes us back out into the great room to a metal door set off by itself. A bright red sign hangs on the door:

GARBAGE DISPOSAL AREA
Danger! Beware of Beast!

"THIS WILL BE AS FAR AS I GO," SAYS THE KEY DROID. "I'M QUITE PARTIAL TO NOT GETTING EATEN, YOU SEE. . . . LAST CHANCE TO TURN BACK. NO ONE WILL THINK ANY LESS OF YOU."

Getting eaten? Man, that droid is really committed to this whole breathworm story.

Dre crosses his arms. "Is there a third test if we skip this one?"

The key droid shakes his head. "AS YOUR GRAND-FATHER ALWAYS SAID, 'IT'S HARD ENOUGH CONVINCING PEOPLE TO GIVE YOU A SECOND CHANCE TO EVER COUNT ON A THIRD.'"

Me and Dre say it too. We've heard that line a million times. We both smile for a second before we catch ourselves.

Dre says, "Just tell us the rules."

"IT'S SIMPLE. MAKE IT BACK WITH THE KEY IN ONE PIECE. NO TIME LIMIT."

"Easy." Dre yanks open the door and starts down the stairs. "Be back in no time."

I get to the bottom of the staircase just in time to see Dre disappear into a tunnel. The place is nothing but tunnels that branch off in every direction. Since Dre went right, I decide to go left, quickly moving from tunnel to tunnel. The smell down here gets worse with every turn.

GRRRR . . . A growl rumbles through the tunnels, raising the hairs on the back of my neck. Man, that was *way* too realistic . . .

GRRRRRRRRR . . . This time the sound is even louder, and, fake or not, I go from a fast walk to a sprint. I round corner after corner, certain I'm going in circles. The light is so dim down here and the smell so rank, it's hard to concentrate.

I'm just about to give up when I trip over something hard and metal. I crouch for a better look and sure enough it's the key. I grab it, the biggest grin on my face, and dash back down the tunnel. No way am I giving Dre a chance to take it from me.

But then I trip over something else. There can't be two keys, can there?

Slowly, I look down at my feet.

This one's not a key. It's a giant bone. A very real bone. And it's got teeth marks on it.

That breathworm is definitely *not* just one of Grandad's made-up stories. And Dre has no idea.

I run as fast as I can down the tunnel, this time *toward* the rumbling echoes.

"Help!" I hear Dre shout as I round the corner to a sight that sends my heart barreling down into my stomach. Dre has been backed into a corner, a hairy green blob slithering toward him. If Big Mac's stories are true, and it sure looks like they are, then that thing could blow its acid breath on Dre at any moment and he's done for.

I think back to how Grandad defeated it in the story. *Two things you gotta remember if you ever get mixed up with a breathworm. First, music soothes the savage beast—that's true on any planet, ya hear? And second, ain't no music more soothing than some classic Motown—also true on any planet . . .*

I clear my throat. I can't believe I'm about to try this.

"*I guess . . . you'd say . . . what can make me feel this way? My girl, my girl, my girl . . .*"

The breathworm whips its massive head toward me and then goes completely still. I can't believe singing the Temptations actually worked! But then the moment passes, and both me and the breathworm realize, at the very same time, I'm no longer singing. It lets out another booming growl and charges in my direction.

"Run, Dre!" I take off, tucking the large key beneath my armpit, the beast right on my heels. I dart through tunnel after tunnel and manage to put some distance between us before I find the staircase and dash up to the door. I give it a hard knock and the key droid pulls it open for me.

But Dre isn't behind me.

Panicked, I dash back down the stairs just in time to hear Dre yell, "Stop!"

And I fear the worst.

". . . *in the name of love . . . before you break my heart . . .*" Dre holds the last note as he inches around the calmed breathworm to the staircase and we both sprint upstairs.

The second we stumble through the door, the key droid slams it shut and locks it tight.

Out of breath, I slump down next to Dre. The two of us lock eyes, and then burst out laughing. Did that really just happen?

"Can't believe you came to help me," says Dre.

"Me either," I say. "I don't know what was worse, that thing's acid breath or your singing."

That has us laughing again.

"Seriously, though," he adds. "Thanks."

"Hey, we're family. I always got your back when it counts."

Dre just nods.

Then he adds in a rush, "I didn't stop caring about space stuff." He hangs his head. "I took the test for space camp too, but I failed. I failed *bad,* man. Realized you have to be book smart to be able to go to space, and that's just not me. I was kind of ashamed to tell anyone. Especially you and Grandad. So I decided to give in to my pops and do what I'm good at. Hooping."

"Come on, you used to be even more into space than

me," I say. "Should've seen how you were cheesing at that model solar system in the main hall. You can't give up on it. Not ever, man."

He lifts his head and grins. "You mean that?"

"Definitely." Now I'm grinning. "But now I gotta claim my inheritance . . ." That's when I realize the key I thought I had all this time isn't there.

"Looking for this?" Dre pulls the long key from up his sleeve. "Must've dropped it on the staircase. Here, man, you deserve it."

I take it, unable to keep the smile from my face. "C'mon, Dre!"

"WAIT FOR ME!" shouts the key droid, waddling after us.

I take a deep breath when I arrive at the golden door. This might be the last thing we ever get from Big Mac. I push the key into the door . . .

And it doesn't work. The key won't twist.

I turn to the key droid, and the thing just shrugs.

"I NEVER SAID THAT EITHER OF THE HIDDEN KEYS WOULD WORK ON THIS DOOR. THEY ACTUALLY OPEN THE POOL ROOM."

"Big Mac pranked us, didn't he?" asks Dre. "Old dude really used his funeral to prank us."

I shake my head. That can't be true. There's got to be something we missed.

Then I think back to that letter, and the answer strikes me like lightning. *I'm putting the key to all my secrets in y'all's hands.*

"Our *hands*—our hands are the keys." I turn to the key droid. "That's why you offered to bring us straight to this door when we first got here. We didn't need to compete. We've had the keys to this door all along."

The key droid does a little dance.

I reach my arm into the lock, feeling around until I find two handles. I grab one and say, "Dre, reach in and grab the other handle."

Dre raises an eyebrow but reaches into the lock with me. We turn the handles in unison and a loud click echoes through the great room.

Grandad's staticky voice sounds through a speaker. "Knew you two'd figure it out. Reckon I really just wanted to say that I love you both, and that spending the summers with you was something I looked forward to every year. Kept this old man young. As long as you two stick together, my memory will live on through you and I'll never be truly gone. Now then, hurry up and decide which one of you is going to inherit the house . . ."

The golden doors swing open.

"'Cause the other gets my spaceship!"

THE LEGENDARY LAWRENCE COBBLER

BY JULIAN WINTERS

"Now add just a pinch of chili powder," says Connie, blue eyes sparkling, smiling like she's won the lottery. "Not too much. We don't want it *too* spicy." She giggles at the camera.

I roll my eyes at my iPad, where my favorite YouTube baker is making a batch of her world-famous cookies.

Chef Connie is always afraid of a little spice. Or too much sugar. Her recipes are really cool starting points, but she's never met a Lawrence before.

We *love* spice and sugar.

I pause the video, writing in the black-and-white journal Mom bought me to keep all my recipe ideas in. I scribble messily, tongue between my teeth, trying not to let sweat rain down on the paper. It's the beginning of May in Atlanta, which means it's eighty degrees outside and one hundred degrees in the kitchen.

It's too early for AC, Dad always says. *Wait till summer.*

I reread my notes.

HOT HONEY PEANUT BUTTER COOKIES

$^3/_4$ cup ~~chunky~~ smooth peanut butter

1 cup honey

1 ~~tsp.~~ tbs. chili powder

I eye the chili powder container on the counter, nodding. "Dad will love this," I say before pressing play on the iPad. Connie goes through more steps for her cookies. She always has this perfect smile and the corniest jokes, but she's super popular.

One day, you're gonna be bigger than Chef Connie, Dad tells me every time we bake together. *A successful, young Black baker with a gazillion followers. Chef Jevon Lawrence!*

I can't help beaming every time he says that. It's one of the reasons I'm learning this new recipe—Dad and I are obsessed with peanut butter cookies. This is gonna be our reward once I win the Turner Middle School Baking Competition.

"If," I remind myself quietly.

Lately, I've been less and less confident that I can win. But that's just the fear talking.

Dad always says, *Fear is nothing but Forgetting Everything's All Right.*

I mean, I've gotten this far. The competition started a month ago with sixteen of us, a big mash-up of sixth, seventh, and eighth graders. Each week, the "judges"—it's just Coach Sanders, a gym teacher, Mrs. Higgins, the school secretary, and Carla Wright, a local TV weatherperson—eliminated four bakers.

And now I'm in the Final Four!

So why am I so nervous?

Honestly, winning feels like the only way to make things go back to normal with Dad, the way they were before I dropped my big secret two months ago. If I win, he'll see me as Jevon, future TV star baker again—not Jevon, his son who said, "I think I like boys" while we made red velvet brownies one Saturday.

I'll never forget Dad's face. He got real quiet. Like, is-he-still-breathing? quiet. He blinked a lot too. Then he whispered, "Oh." And he didn't say anything else as we finished.

He didn't touch any of the brownies that night.

But he helps me practice every week for the competition. He makes suggestions and, sometimes, he smiles so big when I nail a recipe. He's not mad or sad around me—just weird. But weird doesn't feel good.

"Do you smell that?" Connie cheers. "Smells like a winner!"

I nod, shaking those spiderwebby feelings from my head. She's right. Today's going to be perfect. G'Ma is coming over to teach Dad and me how to make the Lawrence family peach cobbler. It's my secret weapon to win the competition.

And then Noah's coming by later. We're going to taste-test each other's final desserts.

I bite my lip. My stomach turns over and over like a washing machine.

Noah Nguyen is a seventh grader, like me. He's my biggest competition too. The guy has his own Instagram for his baking—@sweetnoahbakes—with a thousand followers!

I'd have a big head about that, but Noah's the nicest kid in the entire school. He has this sweet smile that makes the back of my neck warm like laundry fresh out of the dryer. And in the second week of competition, when I forgot to add the brown sugar to my s'mores cookie batter, he reminded me before I put them in the oven.

Who does that?

Last week, as the judges announced the Final Four, we all clasped hands, holding our breath. Noah switched places with Lucy to stand next to me. He grinned, then grabbed my shaking hand. He didn't even roast me for having sweaty palms!

After our names were called, he didn't let go. His cheeks were this bright red and he said, "I'm glad we're in this together."

That's when the swishy stomach thing started.

Which my stomach does right now—in an excited way, not a nervous way—when the doorbell rings.

I pause Connie, then race out of the kitchen. My bare feet *slap-slap-slap* on our hardwood floors. Halfway to the door, I slow down. I'm sweating like I just ran the 100-meter dash. I don't want to be funky when Noah arrives.

Dad exits his "writing cave" to answer the door. He works from home as a comic book writer. It's the coolest thing ever because it means he's free to bake together after school. Mom's busy a lot, being an obstetrician. Turns out a ton of babies are born on weekends or weird hours of the night. Who knew?

The doorbell rings again.

"I'm coming!" yells Dad. He's dressed in his usual clothes: Atlanta United FC gear. He played soccer in college. Dad's super tall, all big shoulders and even bigger leg muscles.

I kind of have his height thing going on. And his dark brown skin. But I'm scrawny, with Mom's tangly curls.

Dad swings the front door open. "Ma! I told you to call me when you're close."

"I know, Junior. But I was listening to my praise and worship and couldn't be bothered."

"It's not even Sunday, Ma."

"So! Every day is a great day for gospel music." G'Ma

struts inside, arms filled with shopping bags. "Help me out, Junior, will ya?"

Dad unleashes his famous grin. It's like vanilla ice cream melting on warm apple pie—perfect! He scoops the bags out of G'Ma's hands and bends down to let her kiss his cheek. "Yes, ma'am."

Then I rush in for the kill. I throw my arms around G'Ma, hugging a little too tightly.

"Von!" she screams, hugging me back. "Baby, you're so tall."

She always says that when we see each other. G'Ma lives in Macon, almost two hours away. She only visits on weekends because of the city traffic.

"Thanks for coming," I mumble into her purple *Lawrence Family Reunion* T-shirt. She smells like spring flowers and those red-and-white peppermint candies.

"Anything for you, Von," she whispers. When I lean back, she cups both my cheeks, her eyes glittery. She looks just like Dad with a few more wrinkles. Well, Dad *before* two months ago. "You're gonna be the Lawrence family's *first* all-star baker."

I grin so hard, I'm afraid my cheeks will break.

"Now." G'Ma wiggles free of me. "Let's bake!"

"Gonna share your secret ingredient for Atlanta's best cobbler with me and Jevon?" Dad asks, his voice booming from the kitchen.

"Not on your life, Junior!" G'Ma shouts back, winking at me.

We both crack up.

While G'Ma unpacks the bags, Dad sets up all the cookware we need on our kitchen island. It's kind of crowded with the peanut butter cookie ingredients I forgot to put away. Dad doesn't complain. He's used to me experimenting with something new in here.

I scribble down every item G'Ma places on the island so Mom and I can go shopping before Tuesday, the day of the finals.

Flour

Brown and white sugar

Butter

Lemon

Vanilla extract

My eyebrows shoot up. "*Frozen* pie crusts?"

G'Ma winks again. "Trust me, Von, baby." She unloads the final item: a giant can of sliced peaches.

"Von, set that oven to three hundred fifty degrees," G'Ma instructs as she yanks her favorite orange apron from her purse. "Junior, we need nutmeg and cinnamon too."

Dad and I move quickly. Once G'Ma is in cooking

mode, it's like she turns into one of those military generals. All bark, no play.

"Wash your hands. Saucepan on the stove. Medium heat." G'Ma ties her apron as we rush around the kitchen. "And for the love of baby Jesus, someone put the AC on in here."

I duck down to laugh quietly so Dad can't see.

"It's not even summer," he grumbles.

"Mmhmm." That's G'Ma's favorite response. It means she's not with it.

"G'Ma, are you gonna *mise en place* first?" I ask.

"Miss-me-who?"

I laugh again. *"Mise en place!"* It's a French cooking phrase for prepping our ingredients that Mr. Conrad taught us at the competition orientation. "Everything in its place!" he had shouted so excitedly, his glasses almost flew off his face.

"I don't know any miss-en-whatever-you-call-it," G'Ma says, dumping the peaches and their thick, sticky juice into the saucepan. "In my day, we just threw it all together and prayed the Lord didn't let us catch food poisoning."

"Maaaaaa," Dad drags out, but he's grinning. I am too. We both love G'Ma's "in my day" stories.

"Zest that lemon, Junior." G'Ma shouts out more

63

directions to Dad while tossing cubed butter in with the peaches, then adds flour. I watch from behind her, biting on my tongue, scribbling away. For an older person, my grandma moves like lightning crackles under her skin. I can barely keep up.

"Wait . . ." I wipe sweat from my forehead. "How much flour? Did you use the whole stick of butter?"

G'Ma shrugs. "I guess. I've made this so many times, I just go with the flow now, Von."

"G'Ma," I groan. "I, uh—"

"Baking is a science, Ma," Dad jumps in. "He needs numbers. Measurements. It's how he puts it all together." He scrubs a hand over my curls.

I smile weakly. Dad always does that—explains things for me when other adults are around. It's helpful, sometimes. But it also makes me feel like I'm five instead of twelve. Like I can't stand up for myself.

"Looks like she used three tablespoons of flour, three-quarters stick of butter," Dad says, waiting patiently as I write everything. "Half cup white sugar, half cup brown."

I nod and nod, scribbling. He gives me measurements for the vanilla and lemon zest too while G'Ma tosses it all in the pan.

"You two make a good team," she comments, dusting her hands on her apron.

I look up at Dad. He's beaming at me, eyes scrunched up. I do the same, even if a little piece of me still remembers what his face looked like two months ago.

G'Ma slides the frozen pie crusts into the preheating oven. "To soften 'em up," she explains. Then she asks me about the competition as she greases the baking dish.

I gush about making the Final Four. I go over the desserts Dad helped me create: no-bake banana-berry cheesecake, the s'mores cookies, root beer float cupcakes. Then I ramble about the other finalists: Farha, an eighth grader whose desserts are as pretty as the hijabs she wears every day to school. Eliana, a sixth grader who killed it with her chocolate tacos in the first round.

Dad stands back, arms crossed, grinning proudly.

"He's gonna beat them all," he says.

When I get to Noah, my voice gets all funny. I'm sweating more too. It's like my stomach is swishing double-time and I can't stand still. I show G'Ma Noah's Instagram.

"Making friends with the enemy?" she teases, ruffling my hair. "He looks like a nice boy."

"He is," I squeak out. I tell her about when Noah helped me. I don't mention the hand holding. I don't know why. But my face gets super hot. Like keeping that from her is wrong.

She nods, smiling softly like she has a secret.

When I look at Dad, his face is blank.

That shame grows in me, branching out like a giant oak tree. My shoulders drop like leaves falling off limbs in November.

G'Ma hip-bumps me. I lift my chin to look at her, making sure not to blink so my embarrassed tears don't spill out.

"You're gonna make all the Lawrences proud, baby," she whispers. Her eyes are a dark brown, but sometimes it's like I can see a million, billion stars in them.

The stars never lie, Mom told me one night. *Trust them.*

I believe those stars in my G'Ma's eyes.

"Now, add cinnamon and nutmeg to those peaches," she says. "I'm gonna start breaking up the crusts, which we'll layer in with the peaches."

I turn away, scrubbing my eyes, then reach out for two spices on the island without looking at Dad.

"How much?" I ask, sprinkling the spices into the bubbling peaches. "Is that too much cinnamon?"

"Von, baby." G'Ma spins around from where she was tearing the pie crust into strips. She clears her throat, then sings, *"It's never too much, never too much . . ."*

And that sets her off. If there's one thing G'Ma loves as much as her gospel music and cooking, it's Luther

Vandross. He's a singer she grew up listening to. I've heard some of his songs. It's mostly slow stuff, but this one song—"Never Too Much"—always gets the three of us going.

G'Ma sings, mostly on-key, grabbing my hands so we can two-step around the kitchen. I think every Black grandma has a two-step living inside of her, dying to get out at weddings and family reunions. Dad joins us, even though he doesn't have half the rhythm G'Ma does. I hope I didn't inherit his bad dance moves. I'd never live that down!

We move around in a circle. Then we do this thing called the "*Soul Train* line" that I see in all the old Black movies. Dad does the running man and G'Ma shimmies and I just hop around on one foot. We laugh our heads off. It's another thing I love about the Lawrences' Kitchen Time—bad dance breakdowns, music, and nonstop laughing.

After we're all sweaty and breathing hard, G'Ma lets me pour and layer the baking dish with syrupy peaches and broken crust. Dad sets a timer on his phone as G'Ma loads the dish into the oven.

"Fifty minutes," she says.

I write that down under all my messy instructions. Mr. Conrad, the eighth-grade science teacher and baking competition host, made it very clear we only have one hour and fifteen minutes to complete our dishes. Usually, we only get an hour. Since it's the finals, he extended it, so "You can produce your best dessert ever!"

I do the math—that means I only have twenty-five minutes to prep everything before it goes in the oven on Tuesday. I need to be perfect.

While Dad and G'Ma are cleaning up and putting away dishes, I spot the chili powder on the island. It's uncapped, next to the nutmeg. I freeze.

Where's the cinnamon?

Did I accidentally use chili powder instead?

I was too busy worrying about Dad's reaction to me talking about Noah. I didn't look at what I was adding.

My heart pounds like a thousand drums. My vision goes blurry like a bad dream. I'm shaking hard.

"Von, baby?" G'Ma calls out, worry in her voice.

But I can't stop the tears once they start.

I hear Dad's voice. "Jevon? Son, what is it?"

I don't answer. My voice won't work, but I'm choking out noises.

Dad tries again. "Jevon Kenneth—"

"It's ruined!" I finally scream. "I used chili powder, not cinnamon. I have to get this right. And I messed up. Noah will be here soon and I'm going to fail everyone." I spin to face Dad. "Especially you."

Dad steps back. I can barely see the shock on his face through all the tears.

"Von, baby." G'Ma's hands grab my shoulders. She gently twists me until we're face to face. "You won't fail anyone."

"Yes, I will." I sniff hard. "Because I like boys and if I don't win, then Dad will—"

"Will what?"

I can't say *not love me*. But it's what I think.

G'Ma frowns. "Baby, you liking boys ain't got nothing to do with how much this world is gonna love you. When I had a girlfriend—"

I gasp, my legs turning to jelly. "G'Ma, you had a what?"

Her whole face glows, those stars in her eyes exploding. "Yes, baby. I dated a wonderful girl in college." She opens Facebook on her phone, then shows me some pictures of her and another girl, hugging and smiling. G'Ma looks at her the way I look at Noah sometimes. "I love boys and girls, Von. Understand?"

I nod.

"Before Papa, there was Liana. I didn't tell anyone about her for a long time 'cause I thought no one would understand or love me. In my day, things were different.

"But you know what? I told your papa . . ." She grins sadly. "And he loved me with every breath. Your daddy—" She points at Dad, who's rubbing his face, looking worried. "He knows about Liana and he's never, ever stopped loving me."

I blink and blink.

G'Ma, the strongest Lawrence I know, is just like me.

"Jevon." Dad kneels in front of me, rubbing my hair. I think about pulling away, but I stay put. "I don't love you any less because you like boys just like I don't love G'Ma any less for who she's loved."

"But—"

He shakes his head, his bottom lip wobbly like he might cry. More tears slide down my face.

"You're *everything* to me. I haven't said anything to you because I'm scared I'll mess up when I do," he says. "That I won't be enough when you need me to be."

"Dad." I hiccup. "Fear is just Forgetting Everything's All Right."

He laughs. G'Ma does too.

"You're right." He kisses my forehead. "The only thing I need to fear is how much more awesome my son's gonna be than I ever was."

I want to call him out. Say that isn't true. But when Dad looks at me, there's a million, billion stars—or maybe tears—in his eyes.

Lawrences never lie.

The timer finally goes off and it's like we're all holding our breath. Dad's the first to move. G'Ma grips my hand with her bone-crushing strength. Dad pulls out the bubbling cobbler and rests it on the island.

It looks delicious. It smells great too. But I can't fight that ugly feeling that it's still ruined.

"I'm gonna try it," says Dad.

"Junior, no!" G'Ma gasps. I try to protest too but Dad's already got a spoon in hand, standing over the steaming cobbler like he's ready to face a monster.

Then Dad shovels a dripping spoonful of peaches and crust into his mouth. He winces, then mumbles, "Itshot!" as he chews. Eyes squeezed shut, his face shifts from pained to saddened.

"It tastes . . ." He pauses to inhale. Then he chews more, mashing the cobbler around in his cheeks. He peeks at me from the corner of his eye. It's torture, the waiting, but then Dad finally shouts, "Spicy! Son, this might even be better than G'Ma's recipe. The chili powder gives it a real kick. I love it!"

I cover my mouth with both hands, but my body slowly relaxes. I've—accidentally—created my own new Lawrence family recipe.

G'Ma says, "I told you. The best Lawrence baker ever!" before doing her two-step.

This is what it means to be a Lawrence: dancing around the kitchen and arguing over the best pairing with the cobbler, which Dad and G'Ma immediately start debating—vanilla ice cream, obviously—and just being ourselves.

The doorbell rings and we all freeze.

That washing-machine feeling in my belly starts up again. But only for a moment.

Dad drops a hand on my shoulder, squeezing, then says, "Noah's here." I swallow, waiting for him to go quiet again, but he doesn't. "I think it's time he officially met the Lawrence family. And he needs to taste this legendary, first-place-winning peach cobbler!"

I smile so hard, even Chef Connie's TV-bright grin can't compete.

FIRST-DAY FLY

BY JASON REYNOLDS

There are only two days that matter to you. Two days that count. Your birthday, which is like a million days away, and tomorrow, which is the first day of school. And normally you don't like school. Because there's not much to like about it. The hallways always smell funny, and they don't do nothing but lead you to teachers. And teachers don't do nothing but remind you that they already got their education and now it's time for you to get yours right before telling you to head back down the hallway to the principal's office because you can't stop talking about how Thomas Baker stepped on your foot with his dirty boots and turned your sneaker into a construction site. Thomas Baker got feet like surfboards. But he don't surf to school. He apparently hikes through a forest that you've never seen around here. Hikes through ditches or something. Swamps, maybe. Anyway, you weren't even talking to no one about him. You were just murmuring *Big Foot Baker* under your breath, bending over at your desk, licking your thumb and scrubbing the brown crust from your babies, scratching the dirt off gently with your nail just like how your mother wipes sleep from your eyes on the mornings you're too lazy to wash your face. You know this is how you bring things back to life. But when it doesn't work, when Thomas Baker's boot mud proves itself to be gold medal boot mud, you decide to attack it with one of the pointy corners of a protractor.

How were you supposed to know geometry is apparently more important than your drip? How were you supposed to hear anything Mrs. Montgomery had to say about triangles and diameters and whatever a hypotenuse is when your sneakers are practically bleeding to death? Bleeding! I mean, can't she see what kind of stress you're under, dealing with such an emergency while also trying to figure out how to use a protractor (who knows how to use a protractor?) and then the rush of hallelujah that comes over you once you realize the protractor is the answer to really scraping the leather clean (*that's* how you use a protractor). Ain't she ever had her fresh ruined? Had her fit downgraded and dismissed because some little boy ain't learned how to use his grown man feet yet? Ain't she ever been through this kind of pain? Maybe she has, but she's forgotten. So Mrs. Montgomery sends you to the principal's office. Again. And everybody moos like cows because they're all immature. Again. And you suck your teeth, but in a mature way.

And that's school.

Well, that's school every day after the first day. But tomorrow is the first day. A day that counts. And you are ready for it. *Ready.* Your older brother has finally given you his favorite pair of jeans, which happens to be your favorite pair of jeans, but when you've asked to borrow them in the past, he's always told you no and he's always said it with bite and growl. Told you they already broken in. Told you the knees are perfect, and you might step in wild and rip the knee from a slash to a hole, and a hole ain't fly. But now he can't fit them, so now he's told you yes. *Yes.* You can't wait. A week ago, you turned them inside out, washed them in cold water, hung them over the shower rod to drip dry because the dryer would turn them into tights. And ain't nothing wrong with tights, but they'd surely guarantee a hole. Somewhere. In the wrong place. At the worst time.

You asked your mother to iron them because she's the best ironer you've ever known. Princess Press. Iron Woman. Can turn wrinkled fabric into something like thinly sliced pieces of wood. She knows how to steam and starch a thing to life. Make it look newer than it looked when it was new. But she said she ain't your maid and asked if you thought the reason she taught you to iron at six years old was so that she could keep doing it for you. You almost sucked your teeth, but didn't, because you love your life and would hate to lose it before the first day of school over a pair of hand-me-down jeans. Instead, you set up the ironing board, put water in the iron, and got to work. First the left leg. You set it flat and press the iron to it and push the button that triggers the steam, causing it to billow out like the ghosts of wrinkles being set free. You have no idea what it's doing—what the steam is really for—but you know this is what you do to make wrinkled things straight. This is ironing. Left leg, right leg. Back and forth across the fabric, steam steam steam. You're careful not to put creases in the jeans because no one should crease their jeans. No one. Not you. Not your brother. Not Mr. Sheinklin, who, for some reason, never got the no-crease memo. Should've been a geometry teacher because his jeans always have the wrongest right angles, and probably some hypotenuses, too. But he don't teach math at all. He teaches . . . you don't actually know what he teaches. But you have him this year for homeroom, and you figure this is your chance to show him what a smooth pair of jeans supposed to look like. Denim like a calm lake, not a rolling river, or a sharp iceberg. Creases are for church pants. And you ain't wearing church pants to school, even if Jesus asked you to.

When you finished ironing them, you hung the jeans across the chair in your room. It's been a week. They're still there. You haven't touched them. Haven't even moved the chair, except for a minute ago when you grabbed the plastic bag from the seat. Something you bought yesterday. Always a tricky experience, moving through the store, past the jewelry counter through the jungle of women's underwear where everything hangs in single pieces, to the factory of men's underwear where everything is folded and packaged like cotton marshmallows. You push a finger through the packaging, puncturing the transparent skin of it, ripping it open before finally pulling a shirt from the strange plastic cocoon housing three of the most beautiful butterflies ever. The white is blinding. You shake the shirt free from its fold, lines cutting through it, a cotton tic-tac-toe board. But, like jeans, T-shirts also can't be creased. Especially not a fresh white. They're supposed to look like this is the first time they've been worn, but not *your* first time ever wearing them, if that makes sense. It makes sense to you. So you gotta get rid of the lines. But not by using an iron. Because it's still just a T-shirt. An undershirt, as your mother calls it. You don't want to take it *too* seriously. So you have to take it really seriously. You put it on a hanger, and hang it on the shower rod, right where you hung the jeans to dry. You close the bathroom door, lock it. Turn on the water. *Hot* hot. Then, sit on the toilet (not like that) and wait.

And wait.

And wait. As steam fills the room, and the creases slowly soften and fall away. Until your brother bangs on the door. He has to go. You tell him you're almost done. He tells you he can't wait. But you know you just need five more minutes, but he tells you he can't hold it. Then you hear another voice, a harder bang. This time it's your mother and she's telling you that water, like money, don't grow on trees, so if you ain't washing your body you need to cut the shower off unless you want to see steam turn into smoke, and you have no idea what that means but you know it would be foolish to find out. Even though,

even though,

e v e n t h o u g h

she was the one who taught you the shower steam trick in the first place. Taught you how to make fresh look like you and not a first day of school costume. But she's still your mother. So when she says turn the shower off, you turn the shower off. There's so much steam you can barely see, but you know the shirt has to be at least close to creaseless by now. You open the door to find your brother bent in half. He's angry but unable to speak. You know there's a punch or something he's saving for you, but you don't have time to stress about it.

Because you still have to get your shoes together. Gotta unlace them, re-lace them, and make sure there's absolutely no evidence of *Big Foot Baker*, make sure his smudge from last year is gone—gone gone—and the creases and wrinkles you've put in these shoes over the course of the last however many months it's been since you got them on your birthday are at least clean, since they can't be ironed or steamed out. You've cleaned them almost every day with toothbrush and toothpaste, rag and soap, and sometimes the sharp corner of a pro-tractor, which is even *more* useful when it comes to pick-ing rocks out the soles.

In your room, you stand in front of the mirror for the dress rehearsal. Because you can't risk it on the day of. You have to run it through. Test it out. So you put the jeans on, pull them up and fasten them around your scrawny waist. They fit you how they used to fit your brother before he got grown. Before the knee slash be-came a thigh slash. You still got about an inch in the waist, and at least two inches waterfalling around your ankles—enough space to be comfortable. Enough space to wear them for a while if you take good care of them. Next the white tee goes on. Wrinkle-free, but not over-done. It looks like you ain't trying too hard to be cool.

To be fresh. You just are because you are. And then, the sneakers. The shoes. The crowns of the feet. Not new, but faithful and dependable when it comes to your fly. Yeah. And you look in the mirror. Like, yeah. And you think. Yeah. You fly. I'm fly. Gon' be fly tomorrow. Gon' put some fresh in that funky hallway. On the first day. A day that counts. Again. And you are ready for it. Again. You, newer than you looked when you were new. And tomorrow, the excitement in the morning will somehow keep you from washing your face. And you will suck your teeth as your mother shakes her head, licks her thumb to clean crust from your eyes. Because that's how you bring things back to life.

Again.
You.

Smile. Because.
You.

know. You   k n o w.
You.

    Will be.
    Fly.   So   *fly.*

GOT ME A JET PACK

BY DON P. HOOPER

"Aw, c'mon, Rod, you know you can't jump that."

I wouldn't have to if Kev didn't kick the ball right over Ms. Wallace's fence—again. But it's my turn to get it.

We always come to the alley off Cortelyou Road to play soccer. It's a narrow, boxed-in space, but it gives us the freedom to practice when the park is crowded. Sometimes there's a wild kick and the ball lands on top of one of the garages and rolls off. Other times it goes into someone's backyard, and that someone is usually Ms. Wallace. She knows my mom and everyone else's fam from church. She always has the biggest smile, especially when she squeezes my cheeks. Don't step on one of her flowers, though, because that smile fades and every Caribbean in East Flatbush will be put on notice until that flower gets justice.

And it looks like our ball rolled over four—nope—six red-yellow tulips.

I do the quick look around. It's only ten a.m. on

Saturday. The curtains over her windows are closed. I can get over the fence and back before she notices.

"Rod, lemme just do it," Kev says. "I'm twice as fast as you, and real talk, you're kinda clumsy."

"Whatever, man," I say. "I got this."

"Don't rip ya pants again," Denton says.

Between the ball and me is an iron fence with a patchwork design that looks like it was made for climbing. My last pair of jeans knows different. I ripped them last month and nobody has let me forget it. My feet are a little big so it's always hard to get a hold. Has nothing to do with me being clumsy.

I grab the top of the fence, stick my foot in, and two moves later, I'm over. Quietest landing ever. I could be a gymnast. The curtains are still closed and no one's out. I rush over to the ball resting comfortably on top of the felled tulips, trying my best not to stomp too hard on the grass and leave more evidence. I grab the ball and toss it to Kev.

"Wow, that's a record for you," Kev says.

Just as I'm climbing back over, my shoelace gets caught on the fence. "Aagh." I topple backward. Kev sucks his teeth.

"Rodney Halfway Tree Clarke!"

The Jamaican accent is unmistakable. I turn around and there she is—Ms. Wallace is ice grilling me from the window. I swear, houses in Brooklyn have the thinnest walls.

I've known Ms. Wallace as long as I've known my parents. And she has just as much power. When she says my whole name, it's trouble. There go video games for a week.

"Later, yo," Kev and Denton say, making a quick exit. Leave it to my friends to break the minute trouble comes. And Kev was the one to kick the ball over the fence!

"Juss hold on a minute right de, suh," she says, her accent magnetically pulling my hand away from the fence, reminding me of the tight network of Caribbean parents in the hood. "Come ere."

I walk to the back door, head down, dreading the one thing I hate most. Lectures.

The door swings open. "Quick, come inside, nuh," she says, doing the same look around I did before climbing the fence.

I can't remember the last time I was inside her house, but the table is filled with grater cakes, gizzada, codfish fritters, sweet plantain, and fried fish. I always thought she lived alone, but she has a feast laid out. I am kinda hungry, but the lights are off, and the curtains are pulled like she's a hermit. The whole setup here is horror-movie creepy.

"We nah haff much time," she says, rushing around her kitchen. She starts dropping Tupperware on the table.

"Yeah," I say, "I'm really sorry about your flowers. It was an accident. Won't let it happen again." I have this speech memorized for these moments.

"Mek yourself a plate to go." She grabs a big black hoodie that looks three sizes too big for me. "You'll need this." She chucks the hoodie at my chest. "It's gonna be cold up dere."

"Really, I'm not that hungry—"

"Put it on!"

I figure I better put the hoodie on 'cause she's already upset. It looked big before, but once I pull it over my head, it fits like it was made for me.

"My mom's expecting me home." No response. "Got math homework to finish." I start reaching for every excuse possible. "And I'm supposed to pick up the laundry. The dry cleaning." Still nothing. I'm pleading. "My dog's been throwing up." I don't even have a dog! No laundry except the pile under my bed. And my homework, I don't really have to finish it. My mom is a research scientist for some nonprofit group. I grew up around math, so algebra takes me like five minutes.

"Yuh mom's already gone. She'll meet us dere."

"Meet us where?" I suck my teeth, groaning. "She said she was going to the supermarket but she'll be back." Pretty sure Ms. Wallace done lost it. I need to get out of here.

She grabs something that looks like a book bag made out of tinfoil and gives it to me. "Put it on." For a moment, my eyes are fixed on the bag. It's like liquid mercury, the kind the second terminator was made of.

This is getting *weird*.

"Look, I just wanna go."

"Me nuh haff time fi explain. We don't know what happened to yuh fadda." She pulls out a large crystal that begins reflecting every color of the spectrum. "We lost track of him before di last race. Yuh mudda went off world to go an find him."

Okay, I gotta get out of here. I lunge for the door. The handle slips through my fingers like air. I grab it again. Nothing. The floor begins to fade, the light from the crystal grows until it's so bright, I can no longer see. Then—

We're inside the crystal. Floating. I see Ms. Wallace's house below me. Then East Flatbush, then Brooklyn, New York, Earth. My head is spinning and I'm happy I didn't eat 'cause I wanna hurl. I don't know if I can't hear myself scream or if I've lost the ability to scream. I don't think I've ever screamed before, but now would be the time. And I can't.

Space. We're in freaking *space*.

I stare around the glasslike spaceship that's been transporting us. We're zooming through a waterfall of starlight in the blackness of space. It's beautiful: endless wonders and radiant colors that can never be captured in a photo. Every few moments the ship makes a gentle booming sound, like a wave crashing against the beach. There is a pulsating flash and we're in a different part of space.

Ms. Wallace grabs my shoulders. "Yuh parents neva told yuh about what dem really do."

"My dad works for the city." The words barely squeak out. "My mom is in research."

She laughs.

"Yuh fadda is a Sundasha and yuh mudda is one of di engineers. Him went off world for the tournament but we tink one of di udda teams nab him up."

My father is a Sundasher? *What??*

"N—no, nah. He went to Jamaica to visit Aunt Di." He just left last week. He travels all the time for work. Maybe I'm trying to convince her or myself. I don't know.

"Yuh auntie is a Sundasha too."

Ms. Wallace breaks it down. Apparently, my dad and aunt are part of some intergalactic racing team. Except, instead of racing for prize money, the Sundashers race to settle disputes between rival galaxies and planets. My dad's team disappeared before the next race and if he doesn't show up, Earth could get invaded along with some planet called Trilark and a few others.

And I have to stop it from happening.

I have to take his place in the race.

"Why me?"

"Intergalactic contracts are signed in genetic code. Only someone with yuh fadda's genetic code can tek him place in di race."

"I'm not even that fast."

"Yuh nah haffi be fast, yuh juss haffi tink fast." She points at the book bag I've been holding on to. "Dat is one a di jet packs yuh mudda design. The hoodie will keep yuh warm as yuh fly and will provide yuh with oxygen once we step out di vessel."

I don't know how long we've been traveling, but the spaceship narrows in on a planet with a blue and red atmosphere. We touch down in the middle of a sapphire canyon with blue rock spires that shimmer into the red mist sky. There are round tents everywhere like a pop-up village.

Kev and Denton would flip if they saw this.

"Put di hood over yuh head," Ms. Wallace says. "It will help yuh breath."

I pull the hood over my head and a light washes over my face like a translucent oxygen mask.

Ms. Wallace walks me over to a yurt that has these retro convertible cars on either side with no wheels. The flap of the yurt opens up and I'm engulfed in Mom's hug. I'm shocked and comforted at the same time. She's really here. A small part of me still thought Ms. Wallace was crazy. I don't remember the last time Mom and I hugged each other like this. But after space travel, a hug is kind of needed.

Mom kisses me on the forehead, seeing the apprehension engraved on my face. I remember when she used to bend down to kiss me. After this summer's growth spurt, I'm nearly her size.

"Rodney, did Simone fill you in?" she asks me, referring to Ms. Wallace.

"Yeah," I reply.

Two squid-like people with tentacles coming out of their noses walk out of the yurt. They're about my height, leaking gelatin ooze as they walk.

"Dese are di Trilarkians," Ms. Wallace says. "Memba what I told yuh. Dere planet is also in danger."

I frown.

"Gurglurgg lurg drgg brugggurg," the purple one says.

"Blugg rlg urg gurglurgg burg," the green adds.

"Your hoodie is in tune with your biorhythms, same

88

as your jet pack," Mom says. "They're speaking Trilark-ian. Empathy drives the hoodie. You just have to want to understand their language, and you'll understand it and speak it."

I'd think this were a dream if each of my senses weren't on fire. Despite the volcanic sky, the air smells like the eucalyptus plants my mom brings home. None of my dreams have ever been this vivid. The air, the can-yons, my mom's hug—they're all real. Even these two squids. No, Trilarkians, my mom said. They're wearing hoodies. They remind me of my friends back in Brook-lyn. *I wonder what Trilarkians are like?*

"Whatup, yo!"

Did the green one just say whatup?

"Call me Kaz," it says.

"Hey, I'm Turin," the other replies.

They dap me up with their tentacles. Who knew aliens were this cool? But I guess my mom hangs with them so maybe they've picked up some things—and I guess if we're in space, we're all aliens.

"I'm going to leave you with Kaz and Turin," Mom says. "There's so much I want to tell you. But the race is starting soon and we have a lead on your dad's loca-tion." She signals to Ms. Wallace. "We think the Metal-loids took your dad. They have the most to lose if he wins the race."

"Mom," I say as she turns to go, "you can't leave. I don't know what I'm supposed to do."

"I'm sorry we don't have more time," she says. "I know you'll figure it out. It's just like any of the equations we work on at home." She and Ms. Wallace jump into one of the wheelless cars. It hovers above the ground and speeds off.

"So you've really never used the jet pack before?" Kaz asks. "Your mom designed this one."

"Well, you gotta be good," Turin says. "Your dad is one of the top Sundashers in Sector 309."

"The story about how your dad saved the Trilark ambassador from Preems moon internment camp is *legendary*."

It seems that everyone knows about my parents but me. Kaz and Turin usher me over to the starting line. But the pressure—of my parents' achievements, of saving some part of the universe I didn't even know existed—is getting to me.

I watch the crowd build. All types of space beings are present. Most are humanoid like the Trilarkians. The Felids look like a mix of panther and tiger. Then there are the Shylites; you don't see them so much as you feel them. They're like walking music notes, speaking through the rhythms of their movements. Finally, there are the Metalloids, robotic creatures with wiry bodies, purple orbs for eyes, and tiny bolts of lightning trickling along their joints. Mom said they might be the ones responsible for taking my dad.

Some are using hovercrafts like the one my mom and Ms. Wallace have, just not as cool. Others have motorcycles with wings. The Metalloids can merge with their ships that look like floating swords with laser-like engines. I'm the only one with a jet pack that looks like a book bag. *What an L.*

The judge starts scanning everyone to make sure they are who they say they are. "So, you're Action's offspring?"

"Who?" I ask.

"That's right," Kaz jumps in. "This is Action Clarke's son, top Sundasher on Earth, second only to Action. Metalloids got nothing on him."

People call my dad Action in space? Great. Dad used to DJ under the name Action Clarke. I guess that's his racing name too. And Kaz is big'n me up like we about to jump into a freestyle battle or get into a one-on-one game on the court. Could someone just give me an instruction manual on how to use this jet pack already?

"What do they call you?" the judge asks.

"Halfway Tree," I reply. They're my middle names

and the place in Jamaica where my parents first met. Cats at the barbershop always called me Halfway Tree, so I figured if my dad's got a tag name, why not me?

Everyone steps up to the starting line.

"Earth is ours," the Metalloid crunches, side-eyeing me with those purple orbs.

If they were trying to make me nervous, it worked. I wanna break out. Head back to Brooklyn. But my mom, dad, Earth. Everyone is counting on me.

"Remember," Turin says, "the jet pack works on thought. You just have to will it to do what you need."

"The more you push your limits," Kaz adds, "the farther it will go. We'll be able to communicate with you through your hoodie comm to give you any tips."

"And don't worry if you crash," Turin says. "The hoodie covers that too. Well, it should." Turin makes a sound like a laugh, and I wonder if that was sarcasm.

The judge signals for everyone to take their mark. My heartbeat kicks up. My throat is dry. I feel like I can't breathe, but I know the hoodie is giving me oxygen. Am I really doing this?

A screeching sound goes off, and the race is on.

Well, everyone else is off. I'm still standing here, looking around like a fool. So I start running. When I play soccer, I'm either the midfielder or winger. I take on the defenders and I attack the goal.

The minute I think of goal, my hoodie generates a digital image of the goal line in front of my face. Now I have a target. I start running toward it, seeing the map of my opponents, tiny moving dots in the distance. It's like the heads-up display in a video game.

But this isn't soccer. No team. Just me and the field. So I push myself. I feel my feet getting lighter and lighter.

And I'm running on air.

"What the—"

I trip over red dust clouds, tumbling back to the ground. Turin was right. I didn't feel anything. This hoodie is awesome. I start again, running, now flying. *This must be what a bird feels like.*

I can see the other racers light up in my display. I gotta catch up. So I do what anyone who's watched a superhero movie does, I reach forward and try to fly faster. No luck. It's more like I'm hang gliding. The dots on the display are getting smaller and smaller. If this were a soccer field, my opponents would be almost at the midfield line. I have to go faster, attack the goal.

Why didn't anyone ever teach me how to do this? And will these Metalloids really invade Earth if I lose? I push the thought aside. That's how you get scored on in a soccer match.

"Dude," I hear Kaz's voice in my head. "You're dead last."

"I know," I scream.

"Aggh," Turin says. "No need to scream. We can hear you."

What did Mom say? It's just like one of the equations we work on at home. In algebra, you solve for a missing variable. The only thing missing now is speed. I just want to GO!

BOOOOM.

An explosion channels me forward. The jet pack is ignited. I feel my entire body on fire with excitement.

"GO!"

I yell it again—free of all limits. This isn't like the alley on Cortelyou. The whole world is my field! I charge ahead as if this is the World Cup and I'm going for the game-winning goal, ripping through webbed trenches and caverns, the defenders who can't stop my flight. My fist is forward. I'm representing for my entire family, friends, Brooklyn, Earth—racing to save the world. Gone are the nerves. My chest is pounding, my body is on fire from the speed and exhilaration. *I gotta get a jet pack for everyone on the block!*

The dots on my HUD are getting bigger; I'm rapidly gaining on my opponents. I whip past one racer, then another. I can see the faint outline of the Metalloid. I'm not far off. I gotta hustle, push myself to fly even faster.

Zzzzt. Zzzzt.

What is that sound?

KRAKOOM.

I glance around my HUD. Two racers disappear from the field. *Did something happen?*

I sense an alert go off, like a defender is charging me from the right. I quickly shift my body, just in time to hear another explosion. On my left, I see smoke. There is a Metalloid racer on my right firing at me. This one isn't officially in the race so it's not showing up on the HUD. But my hoodie is alerting me to the movements, like radar interacting with my skin. I adjust quickly, dribbling down the soccer field, dodging laser fire from all angles, flying through a lightning storm of attacks.

"Beat dem!" My father's voice rings in my head.

"Dad!" I yell, my heart bursting with joy and an ear-to-ear grin on my face.

"We found your dad," Mom says on my hoodie comm. "Now win the race!"

Mom did it. She saved him. That's all I needed to hear. A surge of energy gushes through my veins that I've never felt before. It's up to me now. I'm Action Clarke's son. My mom designed a *jet pack* and rescued him! I got to show them what I can do. I keep my head down and push forward. There are only two racers between the goal and me. I fly past the Shylite racer. All that's left is the Metalloid.

No.

There's just the finish line. I'm racing forward to my parents, the goal, listening to every sense in my body, dodging laser fire, until—

I cross the line.

"And the winner is . . . Halfway Tree of Sector 309!"

"Woo-hoo!" I scream, hearing the announcement, doing aerial somersaults. I wipe my eye, laughing through a mist of happiness. My parents, Ms. Wallace, Turin, Kaz, and other Trilarkians are waving up at me. I savor this moment in the sky, taking in the eucalyptus-scented air, letting the thrill wash over me as I wave to everyone. Then I descend into their embrace.

Flying became second nature; landing, however, is a different story. I tumble to the ground. The crowd picks me up. Everyone is clapping me on my back, shaking my hand, cheering. I'm in a daze. I've never felt like this before. I can't lie. It feels great.

"Yuh didn't juss save Earth," my dad says, holding me in the biggest bear hug. "Yuh save di whole galaxy."

"I guess I'm a Sundasher now too," I say, smiling.

And that's how a Saturday-morning soccer game in BK ended. Who knew jumping a fence could start a whole adventure? Everybody should have a jet pack.

EXTINCT

BY DEAN ATTA

TODAY

I *wake up with a picture*
in my mind of a Nodosaurus,
a heavily armored dinosaur
with bony plates across its back.

I *found out about it when*
I *was looking up extinct animals*
when we got home yesterday.

I *only got to spend an hour*
on my tablet before bedtime.

If I *was allowed,* I *would have*
stayed up all night reading
about all the extinct animals.

The very first thing I *plan to do*
when I *get to school today*
is tell my best friend, Javier,
and my teacher, Mr. Nasir,

everything I learned yesterday
at the Natural History Museum.

Mr. Nasir always says to our class:
"You teach me as much as I teach you."

I'm sure he doesn't know about this.

When I get out of bed,
I check my backpack
to make sure the postcard is still there.

I run to the kitchen, where my big sister,
Tabitha, has a bowl of cereal waiting,
and the milk carton next to the bowl.

She knows I like to pour my milk
because I like my cereal crunchy.

Everyone calls Tabitha "T."
My name is Dylan, but my family
sometimes calls me "Dilly,"
which sometimes annoys me
because it sounds like "silly."

"Good morning, Dilly,"
says T, putting on eyeliner
using her little pink mirror
with the gold bumblebee.

I'm not even annoyed
because I'm so excited.

T wears a lot of makeup.
She's pretty without it,
but she says it's like her armor.

Like a Nodosaurus
or a Stegosaurus.

Stegosaurus *armor*
was flame-shaped spikes
shooting out of its back.
They were to keep it safe
from other dinosaurs
that would try to eat it.

Stegosaurus *and* Nodosaurus
were both herbivores,
which means they ate plants.

Another similarity with T:
she has a "plant-based diet."

She doesn't even drink cow's milk;
she has oat milk on her cereal.

After breakfast,
I double-check my backpack
to make sure the postcard is still there.

It has a picture of a dodo on the front,
and on the back, I've written
important facts I want to tell everyone.

The important facts are:

*"Dodos were flightless birds, like penguins,
but their closest living relatives are pigeons
and doves. Dodos are extinct, which means
there are no more of them alive, anywhere.
The last confirmed sighting of a dodo was
in 1662, which is three hundred and fifty-nine
years ago. According to the United Nations—"*

"Hurry up, Dylan," shouts T.

*When I'm washed and dressed,
I triple-check my backpack
to make sure the postcard is still there.*

*"Let's ride our bikes," says T.
"I think we'll be late otherwise.
Promise me you'll stay close."*

"I promise," I say, and I mean it.

*When we ride together, T always
goes in front, which means she trusts
me to follow her and stay close.*

*I take it seriously because roads
can be dangerous. T always waits
for me, if we're going across traffic,
but in bike lanes, T goes fast,*

and I pedal like lightning to keep up with her.

When there's a bump in the road,
you go up in the air for a moment,
you get that feeling in your stomach
like it doesn't know up from down.
You could be flying, you could be
free-falling. It's like a roller coaster.
Even better, because you don't have
to line up like at a theme park
and riding it is free.

YESTERDAY

The Natural History Museum was free.
T and her girlfriend, Laila, took me.

As we were walking around the museum,
a lot of people were looking at them.

Mom used to tell me it was rude to stare.

I wished Mom was there
to tell those rude strangers to stop staring.

T and Laila didn't seem to be bothered.

Laila wore jeans, a white T-shirt,
and a baseball cap, like me.
Laila doesn't wear much makeup.
She wears lip gloss and eyeshadow
sometimes, but not yesterday.

T was wearing a yellow dress
and hoop earrings so big,
I could put my arm through them.
I actually did it, once.
Luckily, T found it funny because
I didn't damage them.

I see T and Laila all the time,
so I was way more interested in the dinosaurs.

Even though the bones don't give
the complete picture. It's amazing
that they are millions of years old.

But the most exciting thing ever
was the moving T. rex.

Its full name, as you probably know,
is the Tyrannosaurus rex.

Even though I knew it wasn't real—
it's animatronic, a mechanical puppet—
I still felt a teeny tiny bit afraid.

I read the writing on the wall
and learned that "rex" *means* "king" *in Latin.*

I don't speak Latin; I speak some Spanish.
In Spanish "rey" *means* "king."

Javi's abuela calls us both
"pequeños reyes."

In English it means
"little kings."

I remember when T made me watch
a long music video by Beyoncé
called Black Is King.
It had lots of people from Africa,
singing, rapping, and dancing,

and audio clips from The Lion King.
The whole time I was thinking:
Why can't we just watch *The Lion King?*

A T. rex's roar is more
frightening than a lion's roar,
but maybe just because it's less familiar.
It makes a low rumble
and a high screeching at the same time.

I don't think T or Laila noticed
that I was afraid. They didn't notice
when I kept walking. I thought they were
following me, but they weren't.

That's when I stumbled across
the dodo in its glass case.

It was like a small, feathery T. rex,
but it wasn't animatronic,
it was completely still, but something
in its eyes looked almost alive.

But there are no more dodos,
just like there are no more dinosaurs.

I don't know why this was so hard
for me to get my head around, at first.

It looked like it should be alive
in the wild, or at least in a zoo.
Not in a case. Not just a memory.

When Laila found me, she asked:
"Why did you wander off?"

I didn't answer. I was staring at the dodo.
It reminded me of something.

I heard Laila, on the phone:
"I found him, he's by the dodo.
Okay, we'll wait for you here."

Laila kneeled next to me,
I could see her reflection in the glass
of the dodo case, and Laila's face
became her face.

I don't know why but
I decided the dodo was a she.

Suddenly, T's voice boomed:
"Dylan, you scared me!
Don't run off like that ever again.
We don't have to take you out with us,
not if you can't behave yourself."

Then T spun me to face her:
"You're nine years old. You know
not to wander off like that."

I shouted back: "If Dad let me
have a phone, you could've called me.
Maybe you should tell him to get me one."

T folded her arms, and her elbows
looked like the tiny arms of a T. rex:
"Yeah right, as if that's gonna happen.
You're lucky to have a tablet;
that's more than I had at your age.
Trust me, you don't want me
to tell Dad about you wandering off,
or he'll take your tablet away in a flash."

"Go easy on him, T," said Laila,
taking out a packet of tissues
from her pocket and handing one to me.

I didn't realize I was crying.

"I'm sorry," said T, kneeling.
"Were you lost? Were you scared?"

"I guess so . . .
I don't know.
I think I'm sad about the dodo."
That's what I said.

Then T scrunched up her face,
the way Javi always does
when he's trying to work out
a tough math problem.

"What made you sad?" T asked me.

I had to think hard about my reply.
Maybe my face scrunched up as well.

"She's in there, but not really.
There aren't any more dodos
anywhere on Earth."
That's what I said.

"You didn't cry over the dinosaurs
or the—" said T, before she stopped
and hugged me tightly.

She started sniffling,
and I wondered if her makeup
would leave marks on my T-shirt.

I saw over T's shoulder,
Laila had a tissue, too.

I didn't mean to make everyone cry.

When our faces were dry,
we went to the café inside the museum.

Laila and T had their usual:
two fresh mint teas.

I had my favorite: hot chocolate
with whipped cream and marshmallows.
It was like a hug from the inside.

TODAY

I'm doing too much remembering,
and not enough concentrating.

I'm cycling so slowly.

T is waiting at the junction.

I cycle as fast as I can.

When I reach T, she's shaking her head.

She gets off her bike
and leans it against the traffic light pole.

"Oh no, Dylan," sighs T,
"your backpack is open."

I jump off my bike, let it
drop to the ground, and check
to see if the postcard is still there.

It's not!

Did I forget it at home?

No. I triple-checked.

Did it drop out
when I went over a bump in the road?

That must be what happened.

"My postcard," I say to T.
"We have to go back and find it."

"We don't have time, Dylan."

"Please!" I beg. "I have to
show it to Javi and Mr. Nasir."

"There are pictures of dodos online.
You don't need the postcard for that."

"I have to tell them the facts," I say,
"I have to tell them: According to the UN,
up to one million of the estimated eight million
plant and animal species on Earth
are at risk of extinction,
including polar bears,
giraffes, tigers, and Asian elephants."

"Well, you've got it memorized,
so you don't need the postcard."

This time, I know I'm crying:
"I do need it! We have to go back."

"I'm sorry, but there's no time.
I've got to get you to school
and I've got to get to work," says T.

"It's not fair," I shout. "You rushed me!"
I'm breathing heavily.

"I hate you!" I yell.

I don't know why I said that.
I don't hate my sister.

T knows this because
she says: "You don't hate me, Dilly.
I'm your best friend."

I correct T: "My second best friend.
Javi's my best friend."

T laughs. "Fair enough.
You're my second best friend, as well.
Laila's my best friend."

But I think: How can her girlfriend be
her best friend as well?

So I ask: "How can your girlfriend be
your best friend as well?"

T smiles. "I guess I'm just really lucky."

"Were Mom and Dad best friends?" I ask.

"Definitely," says T as she throws her arms
around me. She hugs me, tightly.

Like she did at the museum.

Like she did at the church.

I don't mind
if T gets makeup on my clothes today.

T says, "How about on Saturday
we visit Mom's grave?"
I nod.

I think of the advice Abuela
always gives to Javi:
"El que a buen árbol se arrima,
buena sombra le acobija."

In English this means:
"The one who gets close to a good tree,
good shade shelters him."

I have many good trees:
T, Laila, Dad, Granny, Aunty,
Mr. Nasir, Javi, and Abuela.

Abuela is the oldest.
Not old enough to have seen a dodo,
but old enough to be very wise.

I wonder how wise dinosaurs
would be if they were still alive.

T makes the math problem face again.

"If you don't want to go
to school today, it's okay.

I'll take you back home
and take the day off work."

I put my backpack on.
I imagine it's my armor,
like I'm a Nodosaurus
or a Stegosaurus.

"I want to go to school,"
I say, and I mean it.
"I've got the facts memorized,
so I can still tell Javi
and Mr. Nasir."

"That's a great idea," says T
as she sets my bike upright.

TONIGHT

Mom might not be in a museum,
but she should be remembered.

So I'll make a list on my tablet
of important facts about her.

I already have some in mind:

You always smelled of lavender.
You carried a rose quartz stone.

T says you were the most accepting
mom a daughter could ask for.

Laila says you were like a mom to her, too.
That's something I never knew.

Aunty says you were a protective big sister.
Granny said you were like a rock to her.

I think you're like a dodo
because there isn't another you
anywhere on Earth.

But Dad says the best parts
of you are in T and me:
your feistiness and your empathy.

If what Dad says is true,

I love being like you.

A NOTE FROM THE AUTHOR

Dylan wrote a poem about Mom
without knowing he was doing so.

He made a list of facts,
some he already knew,
and some he researched
by asking other people
who also knew and loved Mom.

If Dylan were to write a poem
about his sister, Tabitha,
he might mention oat milk
and a plant-based diet,
her pink mirror with the gold bumblebee on it,
her big gold hoop earrings,
her being a Beyoncé fan,
her having a girlfriend
who is also her best friend.

Why don't you write a poem
about someone special using important facts
you know about them?

These might include their favorite color,
their smell, an object you associate with them,
and anything else you think is important
from your memory or research.

EPIC VENTURE

BY JAY COLES

Wes sits down at the dining room table in his grand-parents' "mansion." It's not really a mansion, but it's waaaay bigger than the tiny apartment he lives in with his mom. He smiles as he listens to Grandpa Charlie talk about how he shoveled through icy mud and tree roots to dig a hole for shelter to protect himself against enemy fire.

Wes loves a lot of things—comic books, superhero movies, drawing in his sketchbook, and playing *Among Us* with his friends from school—but the thing he loves more than anything in the world are Grandpa Charlie's stories.

Grandpa Charlie is like Superman to Wes. He was a military pilot, fought in wars, lived on every continent, had twelve kids with Grandma Betty—Wes's dad being the youngest of them—speaks multiple languages flu-ently, and he has tattoos all over his arms. When they're together, Wes always begs Grandpa Charlie to tell him more stories: about what his life was like as a kid, what fighting with guns felt like, and even what Wes's dad was like when he was alive, since Wes never got to meet him.

"Would you like some tea, puddin'?" Grandma Betty asks from the kitchen as Wes outlines an airplane soaring in the clouds inside his sketchbook. She's hunched over on her purple cane that matches her dress, her glasses resting on the bridge of her wrinkled nose.

"Sure, Grandma. What kind do you have?" Wes loves tea, but he especially loves tea the way Grandma Betty makes it. She does something to it, like putting her soul into it with a side of honey, the same way she does with everything else she cooks.

"Peppermint or chamomile?" Her voice is sweet, but her accent is hot like the South in summertime.

"I'll take peppermint, please," Wes says. Tails brushes up against Wes's leg underneath the table. Tails is their plump, bright orange rescue cat.

Grandpa Charlie starts his story again, using his hands to mime all the digging he had to do. Wes listens closely and continues sketching what he hears. He draws tanks and military men and the rising sun burning the day away. And when Grandma Betty comes back to give him his tea, his smile doesn't leave his face. He even drinks it with a smile, because this? This is his favorite thing in the world.

"Where were you again?" Wes asks his grandpa.

"Germany," he answers. "Berlin, Germany. Do you know where that is?"

"Yeah! I think so. I could find it on a map," says Wes. "Did you have friends there with you?"

"Of course. I had lots of friends there. It was all of my friends against the bad guys."

"Oh, man. Did you and your friends win?"

"Sometimes we won. Other times, we didn't win. But it wasn't always about winning," Grandpa says, leaning forward a bit. Grandma Betty comes into the doorframe from the kitchen and just stands there, watching and listening.

"What do you mean, Pa?" Wes wears curiosity like a too-tight jacket.

"I mean that it was more about keeping people safe than anything else. You can't truly call something a win if people get hurt," Grandpa answers, his voice a little raspy.

"Oh, yeah. Okay. That makes sense," Wes says and sips his tea at the same time Grandpa Charlie does.

Wes stares at the wrinkles all over Grandpa's dark brown face. Wrinkles around his mouth and on his forehead and around his eyes, and tiny patches of gray hair on his head. Then he asks another question that catches Grandpa Charlie by surprise.

"Grandpa . . . did any of your friends ever get hurt?"

Grandpa Charlie gulps his hot tea and stares at his hands before rolling up one of his sleeves. He points to one of his tattoos.

"You see this?"

Wes nods, eyebrows furrowing.

"It says 'Soldier 12680901.' His name was George. George Salinger. He was my best friend during combat. He had my back, and I had his back. We did everything together. Helped each other with anything. His plane was shot down back in . . ." Grandpa Charlie starts to tear up a little and takes a moment to blink them back.

"Oh, no. I'm so sorry, Grandpa."

"Hey now, that was a long, long time ago. I'm okay. I hadn't talked about George in a long time."

"Was he, like, your best friend?" Wes says.

"Yeah, he was. But you know what? You're now my best friend," Grandpa says, and winks at Wes. Wes offers him a tight-lipped grin.

"What was it like to fly an airplane? Did you feel like Iron Man?"

"Ha-ha. Sometimes," Grandpa answers him. "But more often it was like driving a car in the air through dangerous areas."

"That's so cool," Wes breathes out. "You ever do any tricks with the plane?"

"All the time. Flips, cartwheels in the air, spins, falls, everything. You name it. I've done it."

Wes has to catch his jaw before it falls off. "Wow!"

Wes knows that Grandpa keeps a small airplane in their back garage. "Does your plane still work?" he asks.

"Yeah, it does. I'm actually thinking about selling it sometime soon. I'm only getting older, and it's just sitting in there collecting dust."

"Oh." Wes can't help the pang of disappointment in his chest.

Grandpa Charlie gives him a look. "You know what? I actually want to give it one more go-around before I get rid of it. It's raining at the moment, but I might fly it tomorrow when the weather's nicer."

Wes lights up.

"Would you want to join your old grandpa for his last flight, kiddo?"

Wes can't even get the words to come out properly. "Umm . . . ye-yeah!"

Grandpa winks at him, and they high-five across the table.

"Dinner will be ready in ten minutes," Grandma Betty says, and Wes and Grandpa nod their thankfulness to her. They're having Grandma Betty's famous chicken and dumplings.

Later that night, Wes lies awake in the bed he usually stays in when visiting Grandma and Grandpa, all the lights off, just a flashlight, his pen, and sketchbook. He's putting some of the final details on a sketch from Grandpa's dinnertime story.

Back home, at his apartment, it's sometimes hard for Wes to fall asleep. If it's not police sirens, then it's people arguing right outside his bedroom window. If it's not him staying up thinking about his dad he never got to know, then it's his hyperactive imagination. But here at Grandma and Grandpa's? All of that seems to go away. Something about Grandpa's stories is like taking medicine that actually works—that actually helps him to fall asleep, slowly and then all at once. He's able to dream. Dreams that take him so far away from the life that he knows and into his sketches.

Wes video calls his friends Chadwick and Shawn. He tells them all about him getting to fly with his grandfather.

Moments later, Wes smiles big and shuts his eyes, unable to stop thinking about tomorrow's exciting journey with Grandpa Charlie. Eventually, Wes falls asleep and dreams like he usually does, but his smile doesn't fade until sunrise.

The next morning, Wes wakes up to the smell of hickory bacon and pancakes. Wes washes up, brushes his teeth, and slides into a pair of jeans, a Mandalorian T-shirt, and some Jordan retros he got for Christmas last year.

Tails meets him at the bottom of the stairs before she wobbles herself into the living room to sleep on a couch.

"Good morning, puddin'. Ready to eat?" Grandma Betty asks, wiping her hands on her pancake-batter-covered apron. She brings out a plate for Wes.

"Thanks, Grandma. It smells so good. Where's Grandpa Charlie?"

"He's been fueling up the plane most of the morning and getting it ready to go," Grandma Betty explains. "He's very excited to take you on a little trip. We've already asked your momma and she said you can go."

"Me too," Wes says, and eats a big forkful of pancakes and hickory bacon. Wes wolfs down his food in a flash. By the time Grandma Betty turns back around, his plate is basically empty.

When he's finished, he grabs a jacket and heads outside to the garage. Grandpa Charlie is inspecting the plane, wearing goggles and his baggy military uniform.

Wes looks around, amazed.

Grandpa's garage is filled with old guns, small knives, and other military weapons. Grandpa spent all the years he was in the military and all the years after collecting them, buying them from people all over the world, and going to pawn shops all over the country to find them. Wes has seen them before, but they're secure in glass boxes, which means they're off-limits.

"Ready to burn smoke, kiddo?"

Wes knows exactly what Grandpa Charlie means by that. It's written all over his face. Wes nods and says, "Mm-hm!"

Grandpa Charlie hands him a pair of goggles and some earphones. "Put these on," he says. "It's gonna be loud once we get this bad boy fired up. You'll be able to hear me talking to you through these headphones."

"Okay," Wes says. He stares at the tiny white plane with writing on the side that says Grandpa Charlie's name on it. It looks old and beat-up, like it's toured the world for years and years. For a moment, Wes wonders if it's safe. But if Grandpa Charlie trusts it, then why won't he?

Grandma Betty comes out with her cane and waves. "You two be safe out there! I can't wait to hear all about your trip."

"Love you, Grandma Betty," Wes shouts.

"Love you, too, puddin'!"

Then Wes and Grandpa Charlie climb into the airplane.

Grandpa Charlie starts up the engine of the plane,

and it roars to life so loud that Wes flinches. The propellers begin to rotate slow and then fast, making his eyes get big.

"Make sure to buckle up!" Grandpa Charlie's voice comes through Wes's headset. Wes does as he's told, tightening the strap so there's no way he can fall out of the plane.

Wes stares at all the buttons and switches and lights and gadgets. He's never been in an airplane before, let alone in the seat next to the captain of the plane.

Grandpa Charlie gently guides the plane onto the runway, which just looks like an abandoned track.

"Hang tight!" Grandpa Charlie shouts.

The plane slowly picks up speed and Wes clenches his fists tightly next to him—not because he's scared, though. He's just trying to do everything he can to brace himself for the thrill of a lifetime.

And then, at once, they're off.

Wes feels like he's sinking or falling, even though he knows they're climbing up in the air. His legs are shaky, his hands are cold and sweaty, and his head is pounding, but he's smiling through it all.

It doesn't take long for them to break through the clouds, and when they do, they're soaring soft and gentle, like the clouds are carrying them forward.

"Wow!" Wes says, staring out the window.

"Beautiful, isn't it?" Grandpa says to him. "If I could live anywhere in the world, it would be up here."

Wes silently agrees. He's been to Los Angeles to visit his aunt Ruby and uncle Ray, but they took their minivan, and he's seen photos of some really cool places around the world, but he's never seen anything as beautiful as this. The earth rolling beneath the wings of the plane, clouds of all shapes and sizes looking softer than cotton balls, softer than cotton candy, softer than any blanket Grandma had ever made him. Seeing birds of all kinds soaring from above. Up here, everything is so blue and bright, like Wes imagines Heaven might look like. Wes and Grandpa whirl through the air, but all the earth seems so silent beneath them. It's almost like . . . magic.

Wes wishes he brought his sketchbook to bring back a glimpse of this beauty to Grandma Betty. But also, Wes thinks the reality of being above the clouds is better than any sketch he could ever come up with.

"Everything looks even more perfect from above," Wes says.

"Watch this," Grandpa Charlie says, and the plane tilts sideways. Wes grabs on to a nearby handle and lets out a whoop.

"Whoa," Wes exhales. "So cool, Grandpa."

Grandpa Charlie just smiles and tilts the plane again

and again; each time Wes shouts with more and more excitement. Wes and Grandpa Charlie continue to bob through the air, weaving amongst the clouds for over an hour, before Wes spots snowy mountains on the ground below.

"Are we still in Birmingham, Grandpa?" Wes asks.

"We're hovering over the Appalachians right now. There's Cheaha Mountain right there," Grandpa Charlie points out.

"Have you ever been there?"

"Years ago. I hiked it overnight and nearly passed out when I made it to the top."

"One day, I want to hike that," Wes says, and goes back to staring out the window.

It gets quiet for a moment. There's only the sound of wind pushing the aircraft in the air, making it bounce like a car driving fast down a bumpy road.

"Grandpa, could you tell me another one of your war stories?" Wes asks.

"Of course," Grandpa says with a wide smile. "Well . . . when I was a young boy, I loved reading Buck Rogers and Flash Gordon comics. I had read so many books about the Red Baron. My own daddy would always joke at me that I wanted to fly before I could even walk."

"Really?"

"Oh, yeah. Back during the war, I wasn't eligible to be a military pilot because I didn't graduate college. But the war had gotten so bad that America desperately needed fliers. So, they let me and a bunch of others become fighter pilots. That's when I first met George."

Wes rests his head back and listens.

"Eventually, they shipped us overseas, and George and I were assigned to the 332nd Fighter Group. My plane was called the *Nighthawk*. It was a name George came up with."

"*Nighthawk*. I like that name."

"Me too."

"It sounds like an Avenger."

Grandpa grins. "Well, it was April fourth . . ."

"Mm-hm."

"We were flying into combat against a German fleet. We had destroyed at least two of their planes in the air. We were flying so long in the battle that my legs went completely numb. My butt got tingly, too, from sitting down for so long."

Wes snickers at the mention of Grandpa's butt.

"All of a sudden, a bunch of enemy planes came from out of nowhere and surrounded us. We had to do a lot of tricks with the plane just to escape them."

"Tricks? Like what?"

"Well, like this . . ." Grandpa proceeds to tilt, flip, and turn the plane in different directions to show exactly what he means. Wes's stomach swoops.

He shuts his eyes, imagining how he'd draw it in his sketchbook.

Everything is black-and-white. Wes sees smoke all around him. He sees enemy planes around them, firing at their plane.

Sparks of red and orange and yellow flash before him as bombs release and collide in the air, hitting targets. Enemy planes explode in midair. Some divert and flee.

The colors are so bright.

The planes are so fast.

The clouds are so dark.

The shots are so loud.

Grandpa gives him instructions on how to attack the enemy planes by shooting at them. Wes presses all the buttons he needs to so that they can fire back.

It's only a few minutes but feels more like hours to Wes.

"But then that's when *Nighthawk* was struck by a series of bullets. I could feel them pierce the airplane and it caused us to jerk all over the place."

The plane is going down. Sirens are blaring inside

the aircraft, lights are flashing red, and they're spiraling through the air, thick funnels of black fog around them as they plunge to the ground.

"MAYDAY! MAYDAY! MAYDAY! MAYDAY!" Some siren shouts robotically in the aircraft.

"Pull up! Pull up!" Grandpa shouts to Wes. "Pull up!"

Wes grabs the yoke in front of him, and he pulls up as hard as he can. Grandpa grabs on, too. Together, they're able to stop the plane from spinning and jolting out of control.

"Dang it!" Grandpa shouts.

"What?"

"We're losing fuel!"

"That's not good."

"No, it isn't. We need to get to the ground immediately . . ."

"Okay!"

"Prepare for a hard landing. Brace yourself!"

Suddenly, Wes is pulled back to the moment.

"Whoa."

"Were you asleep?" Grandpa Charlie asks him.

"Um . . . no . . . I don't think so," Wes answers. But as much as it felt like he was dreaming, it also felt completely real.

"Okay. I was just saying that we're gonna turn around

soon," Grandpa says to Wes. "We've gotta head back before it gets dark."

Then he looks at Wes with a gleam in his eye.

"But I want you to help me fly this thing."

"Wait. Really?" Wes's eyes bulge from his head.

Grandpa nods.

"How?"

"Well, the first thing you need to know is to stay calm no matter what."

"Okay. I can be calm," Wes says.

"The next thing you need to do is place your hands on the yoke like this . . ."

Wes mimics holding the yoke in front of him just like Grandpa Charlie shows him. Then Grandpa guides Wes's hands onto the yoke, and just like that, Wes is flying! The whole flight back to Birmingham, Grandpa teaches him about all the different switches and gears.

At one point in the flight, Grandpa looks over at Wes and asks, "What's your dream, kiddo?"

"My dream?"

"Yeah. Every kid has a dream. My dream was to be a military pilot. My dream was to have your dad. My dream was to have *you*."

"Hmm . . . I don't know," Wes says. He's never really thought about it before. There are so many thoughts popcorning around in his brain right now. He's just so glad that he's doing *this*.

"Come on, kiddo. Think about it. What's your dream?" Grandpa nudges him.

"To be like you, Grandpa," Wes answers. And he means it.

They smile at each other for a while, soaking up every part of this moment.

"Well, that's very special, kiddo," Grandpa says. "I'm glad that you want to be like me, but I want to be like you."

"You do?"

"Yep."

"Why?"

"I've seen your sketches. They're so beautiful."

"You really think so?"

"Oh, I know so. You keep it up when you're older, you can be a famous artist someday."

"Thanks, Grandpa."

"Of course, kiddo. I love you to infinity . . ."

". . . and beyond," Wes finishes.

"And beyond that," Grandpa adds, and winks at him.

Eventually they break through clouds and touch back on the ground, landing safely in Birmingham. When they land, his mom is standing next to Grandma Betty, who's holding a pan of something covered with foil.

Once Wes steps out of the plane, his legs wobble like Jell-O and his butt has fallen asleep, just like Grandpa Charlie described earlier.

He runs over to greet Grandma Betty, who whispers that she's made him her famous apple pie and home-made vanilla ice cream. His mom grabs him and hugs him tight, too. Grandpa Charlie comes up behind them with the biggest grin on his face that Wes has ever seen.

Wes grins right back, because he's got his own story to tell now—the story of their epic venture together.

THE DEFINITION OF COOL

BY VARIAN JOHNSON

I pull the pink-and-peach Hawaiian shirt over my head, then check myself out in the mirror. The colors don't exactly match, and my shorts are a little too baggy, but otherwise, I look just like DJ Amplified from Juice Box Squad. I had been planning this outfit for six months—ever since we bought the tickets to the concert. JBS—that's what us superfans call them—always picked people from the crowd to show on the jumbotron during their concerts. This outfit was guaranteed to get their attention. I mean, I'm even wearing socks and sandals—just like DJ Amplified. If that's not dedication, I don't know what is.

I swipe through my phone until I find my favorite song, "Like a Bobblehead," then turn up the volume. It's a bass-heavy song—the type that injects itself into your bones and practically forces you to dance. So that's what I do—I close my eyes, wiggle my shoulders, and tune out everything but the music. And there I am, moving and grooving, jumping and jamming, popping and locking, slipping and sliding, and—

"Des! Did you even hear me?!"

I whip around to face my sixteen-year-old brother, Roosevelt. He's wearing one of his new, overpriced "designer" T-shirts. I won't lie, it looks good—I'd seen Juice Box Squad wearing that logo—but I'm not about to tell that to Roosevelt. His ego is already as big as a swollen mosquito.

"Can we go? Brandy is probably already there. It's almost . . ." He glances at his wrist, then scowls. He stopped wearing a watch two months ago—I guess they aren't "in" right now.

"You mean Brandy and my friend Kordell," I say, following him out of the room.

Well, technically Kordell isn't my friend. Not really. He's just a cool, popular kid who's been in all of my classes since kindergarten—and Brandy's little brother. But thanks to JBS, that's all about to change.

"By the way, I hope you aren't planning to *dance* like that at the concert," Roosevelt says. "You'll look like a stupid nerd."

"That doesn't even make sense, Roosevelt. Nerds aren't dumb."

"You know what I mean. You dance like your arms

are broken. And your shoulders. And maybe your back, too. You look like a stick made of Jell-O."

"You're just jealous because Dad never taught you how to do the King Cobra."

"Ugh. *Please* don't call it that outside of the house." He looks over his shoulder and down toward my feet. "I'm surprised those little twigs you call legs don't—Desmond!" He screeches to a halt so quickly that I almost run into him. "You can't wear that! Socks? *And* sandals?"

I sidestep him and keep right on walking toward the kitchen. "They were good enough for DJ Amplified."

I hear Roosevelt's angry footsteps charge behind me. "Mom! Dad! Tell Des that he has to change!"

Mom and Dad have already risen from their seats at the kitchen table. "Roosevelt, stop worrying about what your brother is wearing," Dad says. "It doesn't matter how you look—as long as you *feel* like you look good."

Mom coughs, clearing what must be a little tickle in her throat. "Are those *black* dress socks?"

I nod. "Cool, right?"

"Of course they are!" Dad says as he reaches into his pocket and pulls out his wallet. "Now, this is just emergency money." He hands each of us a twenty. "And, Desmond, if something goes wrong and you can't find your brother, or if—"

134

"I know, I know." I stuff the money in my pocket. "I'll call you."

Dad strokes his almost fully gray beard. "Maybe I should go up there with y'all. Show you boys what it really means to get down." Dad starts jutting his neck, kind of like *he* was a bobblehead. "Remember how we used to have those dance parties around the living room? Back in the day, I could dance for two hours without breaking a sweat."

Mom rolls her eyes. "That's not what your deodorant said."

Dad isn't paying attention to Mom, though. He's already on a tear. "Shoot, I was so smooth, the word 'cool' didn't exist until I was born. Fellas were just plain corny before that." Dad laughs, way louder than he needs to. Then he slaps his very round belly. "I wonder if they have any extra tickets—"

"Dad, we're going to be late," I spurt out. "My friend is probably already waiting on us."

Dad's eyes crinkle—just for a moment—and then he grins. "Sounds good, slick. Be sure to tell me all about it when you get home."

"Got it, Dad," I say, giving him a high five. Just last year, I was still hugging him. But . . . that doesn't seem to be the right thing to do anymore. I never see any of the other fifth-grade boys hugging their dads. Plus, Dad probably doesn't want to hug me anyway. Whenever I come home from soccer practice, he's always complaining about how I smell like boiled cabbage. I've never eaten it before, but Dad claims that it tastes like soggy celery.

I may have been able to get by with just a high five from Dad, but Mom isn't letting me off that easy. She blocks my way to the door, and doesn't move until I open my arms for a hug.

"Have fun!" she says after a quick squeeze and a kiss on my forehead.

"We will!" Roosevelt says with keys in hand and one foot already out the door.

"Bye," I add, waving to my parents one last time. Mom and Dad wave back . . . and then Dad goes right back to dancing around the kitchen table.

I crank up the new JBS album as soon as we get into the car—partially to enjoy the music . . . and partially to block out all the blah feelings swirling around in my head. Here's the thing: I had watched a million video clips of JBS concerts, and the one thing you never saw in the crowd was parents. Especially parents like my dad, who thinks he's fifteen instead of forty-five. Who thinks dressing up means wearing skinny jeans and retro sneakers. Who likes to dance to both old eighties music and the cool new music that my friends listen to.

So when I heard Kordell talking about the concert earlier this year, I knew I had to get tickets . . . and I knew I had to go with someone *cool*. Enter Roosevelt. He didn't want anything to do with the concert at first—until he learned that Brandy, his long-term crush, was taking Kordell. Then Roosevelt suddenly got super gung-ho about it.

I wasn't really sure how Dad felt about me going with Roosevelt—I kind of asked Mom while Dad was gone on a business trip. But he seemed to be all grins later when we talked about it, so I figured he probably didn't want to go in the first place.

I mean, Dad may be a great dancer, but honestly— I can*not* take him to a JBS concert. He understands that, right?

I'm so deep in thought, I don't realize that we're at the civic center until Roosevelt is turning into the parking lot. He pulls into the first available spot, then checks his phone. "Brandy's waiting on the east side of the building."

As we snake through the parking lot, I check out some of the other people there. Most are kids around my age—though some are a little bit older. And some even have their parents tagging along. *Poor suckers.* As much of a pain as Roosevelt can be, he comes in handy every now and then.

Once we round the building, I see Kordell and Brandy.

Then I notice Jacob, another boy from my class, and his older sister. And then I spot the Gaines twins, Willa and Max. They went to my school last year but are now in middle school. The closer we get to them, the more and more kids I recognize.

I slow down and quickly nudge Roosevelt. "Are we sitting with *all* of those people?" I figure that there are at least six kids there who are around my age. But out of all of them, I only really know Kordell—and just barely. The others are way too cool for me.

"I guess so," Roosevelt replies after a moment. "Brandy said that we might be sitting close to some of her friends . . . but I didn't realize it was *that* many."

Brandy waves at us as we approach. "Hey, Roosevelt! Isn't it cool how we're all able to sit together?" But instead of waiting for his reply, Brandy turns to me. "And hi, Desmond!" Her mouth breaks into a huge grin as she looks me up and down. "That's an . . . um, *interesting* outfit."

I tug at my shirt so she can get a good view of it. "Yeah! I figured I'd dress up, since your brother was, too . . ." I trail off as I get a better look at Kordell. He's wearing a T-shirt. And jeans. And sneakers.

And white socks.

"I . . . I thought you said you were dressing up," I mumble to Kordell.

As soon as he catches sight of my sandals, he clamps his hand over his mouth, like he's trying to contain a laugh.

It's not working. Not at all.

"Be nice, Kordell," Brandy warns. "Don't forget what Mom said."

That does the trick—he finally stops laughing. Well, he finally stops laughing *so much*. "Dude, were you eavesdropping on me or something? I was just joking with my friends when I said I was going to dress up." He shakes his head. "I mean, JBS doesn't even dress like that anymore."

"I think Desmond looks adorable," Brandy says. "And who knows—maybe he'll end up on the big screen because of his little outfit."

Ugh. *Adorable.* That's what Mom says about the ugly Christmas sweaters Aunt Amber sends us every year. But at least Brandy gets that I'm trying to get on the jumbotron.

As we enter the building, I discover that Brandy was in charge of coordinating seating with all her high school friends and their younger siblings. We're all in a little cluster—with me and Roosevelt along with Brandy and Kordell in one row, three other groups on the row behind us, and two more on the row behind them. The teens are trying to be all sophisticated, talking about movies and sports teams that no one cares about, while the rest of us stuff our faces with popcorn and soda. If the other kids are like me, they're trying to get their eating in now, so they can dance later on.

There are two warm-up acts—a juggler and a clown who likes to get pies thrown in his face. It takes *forever* to clean all the whipped cream from the floor.

But as soon as they're done, glitter begins to fall from the ceiling. And not just any glitter. It's red, yellow, and green, the official JBS colors. As I lean forward—hoping, praying, *wishing*—the arena starts to chant and cheer.

Everything goes dark.

Everyone cheers louder.

Then the lights flash back on, and there they are!

Juice Box Squad!

The crowd erupts as DJ Amplified kicks off the track from their newest song. There are three other singers in the group, but to me, DJ Amplified is the biggest star. He holds his headphones to his ear with one hand while working the turntables with the other—controlling the beat as the rest of the group sings.

Except . . . his actions aren't totally in sync with the

music. It's like he's a half-second slow sometimes. And then, right in the middle of the next song—when the track switches to one of those old-school beats that Dad loves to talk about so much—well, his hands aren't even on the controls when the music changes. He's too busy readjusting his glasses.

But I don't have time to worry about that, because Jilly the Filly from JBS starts yelling, "You know what time it is, right?! Who wants the spotlight?!"

That's my cue! I jump up, and as DJ Amplified—or whoever is behind the scenes—plays the next song, I launch into my dance. Every few seconds, I peek at the jumbotron, but it's always showing someone else. Still, I keep dancing, figuring that they'll eventually find me and my awesome outfit.

"He looks like a fool," one of the girls says behind me.

"OMG! He is so embarrassing," Willa says next.

I glance at the jumbotron, curious to see who they're making fun of. But the screen is back on Jilly the Filly.

I turn to Roosevelt. "Who was on the screen? What was so funny?"

He quickly shakes his head. "It was nothing. But, um, maybe you should sit down."

"No way!" I pump my arms harder. "They're still showing people on the—"

"Desmond! Look at me!" Jacob yells.

I spin around—and see Jacob Clemmons holding up his phone. Filming me.

"This is hilarious!" he says, his eyes locked on the screen. "Wait till I show everyone at school!"

I look around and notice that two other kids are recording me as well. Even Kordell is fumbling to get his phone out of his pocket.

And with all that going on, it still takes a second for me to realize that I'm still dancing. Still doing the stupid King Cobra.

And they're all still laughing.

I finally force my feet to stop moving, and a second later, the tears begin building in my eyes. Maybe Roosevelt notices this as well, because he quickly scrambles out of his seat. "Want some popcorn?" He grabs my arm. "Come on."

Roosevelt pulls me out of the row and up the stairs toward an exit. I don't know where we're going, but anyplace is better than staying in that arena.

He stops once we reach the concessions level. "You okay?"

I keep my gaze down. Those tears that had been working their way to the front of my eyes now begin to fall. I watch as the teardrops splash against my dusty sandals.

"Des?" he asks. "Say something."

I shake my head. There's no way I can look at him right now. I'm afraid that I'll catch him shrugging, like I should pretend that this is all a big joke. Or worse, he'll smirk and say, *I told you so.*

But instead, he quietly says, "How about we find a bathroom."

He offers to go inside with me, but I tell him I'd prefer to go in alone. I quickly enter the first stall, then lock the door behind me. The tissue feels like sandpaper, but it's good enough to dry my cheeks and nose. Then I check my watch and wonder if it's too soon to go home.

I exit the stall as two old men enter the bathroom. Actually, it's more like they *dance* into the bathroom. Or *strut.* Or even *jitterbug.*

And when I say old, I don't mean my parents' age. I mean, like, *really* old. Like—*grandparent* old. Like the kind of old people who yell, "Get off of my lawn!"

But . . . they were also wearing skinny jeans and Jordans. And they're rocking freshly cut fades—with what little hair they have left.

"Hurry up, Frank," the taller one says to the other. "We're missing the good stuff."

"You know my bladder ain't what it used to be."

"Then you shouldn't have drunk all those sodas. You know it's not good for your diabetes—"

"Pre-diabetes, Herman. Don't put me in the grave yet."

I begin to laugh but quickly bite down on my lip. Herman narrows his eyes at me. "What's so funny, whippersnapper?"

"Nothing, sir," I mumble as I erase the grin from my face. I walk to the sink and begin washing my hands. "Are you here with your grandkids?" I ask, trying to make small talk.

"Shoot, no. My grandkids are in their forties. I'm here with my *great*-grands."

Oh, wow. Those kids must be so embarrassed. And I thought *my* day was going bad.

"I think it's really nice that you came out with them," I say, hoping that he can't tell what I'm thinking. "Is it too loud out there for you?"

"You kidding? I want them to pump up the volume more. Dancing ain't dancing unless you can feel the music in your bones." Herman pulls a handkerchief from his pocket and wipes his brow. "I know we look a little out of place, with all you young'uns, but shucks—age ain't nothin' but a number. And I'd do just about anything to spend time with them kids—even though they're spoiled rotten."

"Rotten to the core," Frank yells from the stall.

"Stop talking about my grandchildren like that,"

Herman says. Then he shrugs. "My brother is right about them being spoiled, though. They're so busy trying to be hip and cool, they're missing out on all the fun."

"That's too bad for them," Frank says as he opens the stall door. He does a little shuffle on his way to the sink, and adds, "But they ain't gonna mess up my groove."

"Will you hurry up? I'm trying to get on that jumbotron." Herman looks at me. "Seems like you're trying to get on there as well."

I look down at my clothes. "Yeah, I am. Well, I was."

Frank laughs as he dries his hands. "What? You too *cool* to dance? Shucks—that just gives us more opportunity to get picked." He winks. "Good luck, slick."

Slick. That's what Dad calls me when he's joking around. And dancing. And having fun.

As I follow the men out of the bathroom, I think about how I laughed at them. How I cringed at what they were wearing.

I was just as bad—just as *cool*—as Kordell.

"Des?" Roosevelt walks up to me with a frown on his face. "What were you doing in there for so long? Wait, I don't want to know."

"Stop playing," I say, nudging him. "I was just wiping my nose."

He stuffs his hands into his pockets. "So now what? Want to go home? Or maybe we could go to a restaurant or—"

"We should go back."

He eyes me again. "You sure?"

But I was too busy walking toward the stairs to respond.

No one says anything to us as we slip into our seats. Juice Box Squad is still going strong, playing hit after hit. I really want to get up and dance, but, well . . . I'm not brave enough for that. Not yet. I wish I could be like Herman and Frank. I wish I could be like my dad. I wish—

"Do you all want one more chance to be famous?!?!?!?" I turn to the stage to see DJ Amplified yelling into the microphone. Then he presses a button on his computer, and "Like a Bobblehead" cranks through the speakers. "Get up and show us what you got!"

I quickly glance at everyone else in our group. Kordell is dancing a little in his seat but stops when Jacob catches sight of him. Max and Willa are nodding their heads a little, but that's it.

I think about what Herman and Frank would say to me. I think about what Dad would say.

They ain't gonna mess up my groove . . . slick!

Before I know it, I'm on my feet—eyes closed, shoulders wiggling—doing my best interpretation of the King Cobra. At first, I'm barely dancing, trying my best to pretend that no one is looking at me. But as the music gets deep down into my bones, I start moving and grooving, jumping and jamming, popping and locking, slipping and sliding and—

Then someone bumps into me.

I keep my eyes closed and start up again, really pumping my arms this time.

Another bump.

And then another.

My eyes flash open.

It's Roosevelt!

But he's not bumping me on purpose. His eyes are closed, too.

He's doing the King Cobra!

"How did you learn that dance?" I ask.

He opens one eye and bobs his head at me. "Fool! Who do you think Dad taught first?"

Then a spotlight hits us. It's so bright, I have to block my eyes.

"And look at these guys!" DJ Amplified yells.

I turn to the jumbotron, and sure enough, there we are, doing the King Cobra in front of the entire crowd.

I'm sure that some people are laughing at us, but all I choose to focus on are the cheers. And I'm not positive but I think I hear an old voice call out, "Cut a rug, slick!"

Finally, after the spotlight moves on, we drop back to our seats. Someone bumps me again, but this time it's Kordell, tapping me on the shoulder.

"Um . . . what was that dance you were doing?" he asks.

I puff out my chest. "It's called the King Cobra."

He nods quickly. "Do you think . . . um . . . maybe you can show it to me later?"

I frown for a second, ready to turn him down. But then I think about Herman and Frank again. It would be nice to have someone to dance with who was my age. "Sure. Maybe after the concert? Or this weekend?"

Kordell nods. Then he takes a deep breath. "And about before . . . I'm sorry about—"

"It's okay," I say, because it is. And plus, for a while, I wasn't any better than him.

We fist-bump, then turn back to the stage. A few seconds later, Roosevelt wraps his arm around my neck and gives me a squeeze. "I'm proud of you, bro," he whispers. "And while you were in the bathroom, I heard an announcement about Reedy Jay coming to the civic center in a couple of months. Do you want to get tickets?"

"Reedy Jay! He's like my second-favorite singer. Well, third-favorite! And he does these dance moves where—"

"Okay! Okay! We can talk to Dad about it tonight. Though knowing him, he'll probably want to come."

I don't even hesitate. "That doesn't sound so bad."

Roosevelt leans back. "You sure?"

"Yeah." I smile big and wide. "I think it would be really . . . *cool*."

THE GRIOT OF GROVER STREET

BY KWAME MBALIA

PART TWO

FORT STARED at the jar as more tiny bubbles flooded inside. Collecting the joy from the stories had been tiring, and they still weren't done. But it had been fun. Sort of. Different stories held different kinds of joy. The joy of looking fly, of figuring out secrets, of magic. Yeah, definitely the joy of magic. But . . . the boy tried to put his finger on something that confused him. He pressed his face against the glass. "Some of those felt . . . I don't know, kinda sad."

"Of course!" Mr. G propped the butterfly net on one shoulder and leaned against the jar, dropping to sit on the swirling silvery floor, and sighed heavily. "Sadness is but one side of the coin. Necessary. Must be expressed if we're to rediscover the other three sides."

"Three?"

"Fear, anger, and joy. All part of the same four-sided coin."

Fort wrinkled his brow. Another planet was approaching. He could sense a familiar buzzing warmth. The same feeling that came from the jar. Mr. G looked exhausted, so Fort grabbed the net.

"I've never seen a four-sided coin," he said. "Guess I got a lot to learn about the Between."

Mr. G watched Fort twirl the net with a little flourish, handling it in a way that had taken the older man years to master. The boy propped it on his shoulder as he prepared to blow more bubbles at the approaching planet.

"I don't know," Mr. G said, leaning his head back and smiling. "I expect you'll catch on pretty quick."

FIVE THOUSAND LIGHT-YEARS TO HOME

BY SUYI DAVIES OKUNGBOWA

Keziah loved puzzles.

He loved the cryptic ones best—the ones where you had to look hard to find something that wasn't obvious at first. But really, he loved anything that allowed him to think hard and find a solution: picture puzzles, jigsaws, crosswords, Rubik's cubes, riddles, trivia. The rush he felt when he solved one was second to none.

Except math puzzles. Keziah *hated* math.

But even puzzles didn't make up for the fact that his family was moving to one of the tall, lifeless buildings in Willow Island, Lagos, where he had zero friends. Keziah sighed and tucked the puzzle he had been working on—a word search—into the front seat pocket as his mom pulled into the parking lot of their new building. They were going to check out the apartment today, and his parents had wanted him to come along, but Keziah couldn't muster any enthusiasm. He scowled as he slammed the car door shut, and his parents gave him a warning look. At the elevator they met a lady who introduced herself as an estate agent. Keziah had never been in an elevator before, and despite his grumpy mood, he was instantly fascinated by it. How fast could it go? What caused it to make that little bump when it stopped?

It all ended quickly, though, as the doors opened and his parents got out with the estate lady.

"Come on, K," Mom said.

"Can I just keep riding the elevator?" Keziah asked, remaining inside.

"We have to see the apartment," Dad said, standing in the space between the doors to prevent them from closing. "Come on."

"Why do I have to come?" he asked. "It's empty and boring. I'm not going to make any friends here."

"Keziah Anietie," Mom said. She always said his full name whenever she considered his behavior improper. "You come out here right this instant."

So he did. They walked the narrow corridor to the new apartment, which was as bare and boring as he had imagined—how could they be so excited about a place that had nothing in it? The lady kept using words he didn't understand and pointing at things he didn't care about, but Mom and Dad just kept going *ooh* and *aah*. The elevator aside, Keziah wasn't interested in anything about the apartment. Not even when Mom pointed and said, "That's going to be your new bedroom, K, you like it?"

"It's smaller than the old one," he said.

Afterward, the grown-ups went to a corner of the empty living room and began to discuss things in low tones, pointing at one sheet of paper or the other. They were so engrossed, they soon forgot about him. Keziah found his chance and tried the front door. Unlocked.

Slowly, stealthily, Keziah Anietie slipped out of the apartment and made for the elevator.

The corridors of the building were a maze. *How can we live here if I can't even find the elevator?* Keziah thought.

He went around and around, finding only doors upon doors. So he followed the stairs, down, up, down, until he finally found steel-like double doors. SERVICE ELEVATOR, the sign said.

"Finally," said Keziah, and pressed the button.

The machine creaked to a stop before him and dinged, and the doors opened. It was larger and darker than the one he had ridden in earlier. He got in and pressed a button—any button. The doors closed and he began to descend.

This elevator looked way older than the last. Hadn't

been cleaned in a long time, either. And those shiny colors that swirled as he went—was that a thing that elevators did?

The elevator suddenly let out a long groan. The shiny colors swirled, faster, faster. Keziah grew dizzy, so dizzy he found himself floating, weightless, falling. He screamed.

Then the elevator came to a creaking halt and Keziah passed out on the floor.

When Keziah awoke, someone was talking to him.

Wake up, get up, hey! someone was saying, but he couldn't see who because the elevator lights had gone out.

"What happened?" He lifted his head, then slowly got to his feet. "Who's there?"

Psst! Up here! the voice said. Keziah peered through the dimness and saw a lizard—a large red-spotted gecko—looking down at him.

"Are you . . . talking to me?" He paused. "In my head?"

Is there anyone else here with us? The lizard seemed to shake its head.

"No, no, I'm dreaming," Keziah said. "This can't be real. Lizards don't talk."

You better believe we do, the lizard said, scurrying down the wall and jumping into Keziah's pants pocket. *Now look alive, they're coming.*

Before Keziah could respond, the doors opened, and light streamed into the elevator.

At first, he thought the doors had opened into an old part of the apartment building, but the longer he looked at it, the more he became aware he was not even in an elevator, but some sort of cubicle. The large hall before him was ancient and dim, with rusting metal, dripping pipes, and flickering lights. Rows upon rows of cubicles lined the hallways, stacked one on top of the other, with glass fronts. Through those, he could see people—children, just like him, all dressed in the same white uniform. They were reading, sleeping, playing games—but they all seemed unhappy and they didn't pay him any mind.

The woman standing in front of him—was she a woman? He couldn't tell—held a long baton-like instrument. She was dressed in a uniform so prim and stood so straight that she could've been a sculpture. He wasn't sure what to think of her face, but he knew two things: one, she was *definitely* an alien; and two, wherever she was from, did everyone else also look like a crocodile?

"All right, you," she said curtly, her lips curling to reveal a row of pointy teeth. "Out and about, now." She tapped her stick on her legs. "Your number is 1521. Be sure to remember it."

"Number?" Keziah asked, but she prodded him out of the cubicle with her stick.

"Off with you, now, join in line," she said. He stumbled forward and was hustled into an already moving throng of kids who were just as confused, some already weeping and asking for their parents. Their wails echoed off the curved steel walls.

What is happening? Keziah thought, fighting back the cold crawling up his spine. *What is this place?*

Just keep your head straight and look forward, said the lizard in his pocket, who he'd almost forgotten about.

Soon, he found himself in another large room that was covered in doors. Each door had a pair of children in front of it. Keziah was shoved forward toward a door on the left, next to a girl with glasses.

"Psst!" she said when the wardens had left them alone. "Do you know where we are?" Keziah simply shook his head.

"Step through, please," a voice said over invisible speakers. The girl gave Keziah a questioning look, then pushed the door open.

As they stepped through the door, they found themselves in a narrow corridor. A row of lights lit up the darkness before them. A door at the end of the hallway before them slid open to another room just like the one before. This one had a table in the middle, with various shiny, glowing pieces of something scattered over it. Keziah ran over to it, momentarily forgetting about the strange girl and the even stranger place where they'd ended up. On closer examination, Keziah realized they were jigsaw pieces.

A puzzle! Keziah couldn't believe his eyes. Finally, a familiar thing from his real world. It looked straightforward, except . . .

"Where's the picture we need to solve it?" The strange girl next to him shrugged. He looked around for other clues, but there was nothing else on the table.

He heard a click and looked at the wall behind him. A countdown clock had started. Thirty minutes.

"Okay, what's going on?" the girl asked.

It's a trial, the lizard said.

"A what?" Keziah and the girl asked at the same time.

"Who said that?" the girl said, looking around.

Keziah's eyes widened. "You can hear him, too?"

"Hear who?"

Keziah dipped his hand into his pocket, pulled out the lizard, and placed it down gently. "Him."

The girl peered at the lizard and back at Keziah.

"We're talking to a *lizard*?" A small frown played on her forehead. "Where did you find him?"

"He was here when I woke up in this place."

Her eyes widened. "So you mean he's from . . . here?" She knelt before the lizard. "Where are we?"

The Stonehound, came the reply.

"The what?" Keziah asked.

It's a spaceship. Well, it was a spaceship once, but it malfunctioned during one of its flights, and it got stuck here. Now it has been converted to an intergalactic establishment where children throughout the universe are sent when they've lost their way. These trials are a shortcut—pass them, and a portal opens up and returns you home, just like the one that brought you here. But fail, and you remain here for a long, long time, just like others before you.

The girl looked like she was about to cry. "We'll be stuck?"

Yes, the lizard said. *Five thousand light-years from home.*

The kids sat, dumbfounded.

"What did you do?" Keziah asked the girl. "I mean, to get sent here."

"I—I ran away from home," she said, sounding very small. "My best friend moved away from our building, and I was angry."

"I'm actually moving away, too," Keziah said. "To Willow Island. And my parents don't seem to care that I don't have any friends there."

"Willow Island?" the girl said, a funny look on her face. "That's where I'm from." She extended a hand. "My name is Adanna."

"I'm Keziah." He tried thinking back to the lizard: *What is your name?*

I am the Critterling, came the reply. *I have lived in this ship for ages. But you must hurry now and complete the trial before you.*

"Argh, the puzzle!" Keziah and Adanna rushed to the table. But how were they supposed to put together a picture they hadn't seen?

"What is it, even?" Adanna asked.

It is the Stonehound, the Critterling said. *What it looks like from the outside.*

"But we've never seen it," Keziah said.

Then use your imagination.

"Can you imagine a spaceship?" Keziah asked Adanna.

She thought for a moment. "I can try?"

So they set to work. Keziah employed all the tricks he'd learned in solving jigsaws: start from the edges; group similar pieces by color, texture, shapes; look for clues to find where they match. Adanna grouped the pieces while he put the jigsaw together.

The Critterling was right. The edges were dark and cloudy like what Keziah imagined space would look like. The gray pieces were the body, the black was the tail, and the whites were the lights.

"I think . . . that's it?" Adanna said. And she was right—they had finished the puzzle. Keziah knew they had done it correctly, too, because the counter went down, a green light buzzed, and a panel in the wall slid open for them to walk through.

Now listen very carefully, the Critterling said. *This is the big trial. You must understand it will test every single aspect of your wits. No two children have ever been able to solve it.*

"No one?" Keziah asked.

None—and I have followed many!

"We'll try," Adanna said.

"Yes," Keziah said. "We'll get home."

When they went into the room for the final trial, the lights went out and the countdown started in a dim red light. One hour.

"What kind of puzzle is this?" Keziah asked. "I can't even see anything!"

It is not one puzzle, but many. It is—

"A puzzlehunt!" Keziah screamed, then slapped a hand over his mouth.

Adanna raised an eyebrow at him, then giggled. "What's a puzzlehunt?" she asked.

Keziah had learned about puzzlehunts from watching some of his favorite TV shows. In the shows, the kids would race against one another to solve a series of connected puzzles that revealed one final solution or prize. He explained it to Adanna in a rush.

A light lit up on the first puzzle and they sprinted over to it. There was a lone object sitting on the pedestal and a screen with an audio clip. Keziah pushed play.

"This is the black box of the *Stonehound*'s last moments before permanent malfunction," a mechanical voice read. "Most of the data is corrupted. To determine what happened to the *Stonehound*, you must fill in the missing information."

When the clip finished playing, the rest of the room lit up in five different spots, each with a clue material and an audio clip just like the others.

"I don't know anything about flights," Keziah said.

"I do," Adanna said, grinning. "My mom is a pilot. She talks to me about flying all the time!" She walked about the room. "It's like we're looking for five missing pieces of the flight information: mission number, departure, destination, flight path, last known status. We need the first to begin anything."

They headed to the first station, which was not a

puzzle per se but a math equation where they were supposed to solve for a value.

"I don't really . . . do math," Keziah confessed. "I'm not so great at it."

"Oh, that's nothing to be ashamed of," she said. "I'm not great either, but we can try together."

They worked their way through the puzzle slowly, sweating as they tackled numbers in their heads. When they figured out the answer to the equation, they punched it in, and the screen blinked green. They cheered.

The second, the Critterling said. *Go, fast!*

They went through the next three puzzles in the same manner. The second was a word puzzle whose answer offered the departure information of the *Stonehound,* a planet called Castle. The third was something similar to a Rubik's cube, but the arranged letters spelled out the ship's destination, a planet called Liew. The fourth was a pattern puzzle that showed the flight path once they deduced the repeating pattern.

When they came to the fifth and final puzzle, there were only ten minutes left. It was a string of letters with five missing. A message read: *A part of your body that you can never hold with both hands.*

"Your wrist?" Keziah said. He'd heard this riddle before.

"I've heard it's your elbow," Adanna said, peering at the message. "And look, we only get one try."

"And both our solutions are five letters each!"

The countdown's clicks were so loud now. Both kids were sweating.

"How sure are you about your answer?" Keziah asked.

"I don't know," Adanna said. "You?"

"Me neither," he said.

They stared at one another.

"You know," Adanna said. "My mother used to say we make mistakes and learn from them. Maybe making mistakes isn't too bad after all. Getting the best out of them—like making a new friend—is what matters, right?"

Keziah nodded.

"Whatever happens after we choose," he said, "can we still be friends?"

"Definitely," Adanna said.

They turned back to the screen.

"I say we go with your elbow," Adanna said. "It makes more sense. I can still touch my wrist with the same hand." She bent her wrist all the way, laughing and reaching with her fingers.

Keziah grinned and nodded. "Let's do it." He punched the letters and waited, finger poised over the final button.

"Together," Adanna said, and they pushed the button with a finger each.

They winced together, waiting for the red signal to go off. But a green signal went off instead, and the letters arranged to spell another word—BELOW—that completed the information for the ship's last known location. All the puzzles in the room disappeared, the lights came back on, and a door opened into a cubicle.

"We did it!" They high-fived one another.

"Congratulations," a voice said. "You may now exit the *Stonehound*. And may you never return."

Keziah and Adanna stepped into the cubicle, the Critterling in Keziah's pocket. The door shut, and darkness engulfed them.

When Keziah woke up, his parents and the estate agent were peering over him. Behind them stood two men dressed in work overalls.

"Are you all right?" Mom was asking, shaking his shoulders.

Keziah looked around. He was back in the elevator. Somehow, the men had forced open the doors.

"I—I—" Keziah was saying.

"Shh, shh," Mom said. "Let's get you out of here."

Mom took Keziah to a nearby bench and sat with him, rubbing his head. While she fussed over him, Keziah looked in his pocket. The Critterling was still there.

Can you still speak? Keziah asked.

Yes, the Critterling responded.

We did it! We passed the trials! Keziah said.

Yes, the Critterling said. *And for that, I must thank you. You said we would get home—and we did. Because of you.*

And Adanna too.

Yes, the Critterling said. *She, too, is home now.*

Will I see her again soon? Keziah asked.

Oh yes. I hear this is a tiny island, even smaller than the Stonehound*! You should run into each other soon. And as long as I am with you, she can always hear me, and will find you.*

Keziah smiled for the first time since waking up.

"What are you smiling about?" Mom asked.

"Nothing," Keziah said. "I'm just excited to be moving here."

Mom arched an eyebrow. "Really? You were so worried you wouldn't find friends here!"

Keziah's smile widened.

"You know what? I think I already have."

COPING

BY TOCHI ONYEBUCHI

For 2.7 seconds, CJ Walker could fly.

It felt like a lot longer. As the quarter-pipe ramp got smaller underneath him, it started to feel like he was just going to hang sideways in the air forever, fumbling for his skateboard, trying to keep it pressed to the soles of his feet. He was supposed to do other things. He was supposed to twist his body. Left. No! Right. No, he was supposed to curl into himself so that he could flip forward. No, he was supposed to be still. Stock-still. No, wait, he was supposed to—

The first thing he noticed when he woke up: the ground was really soft. Too soft. It felt like . . . a mattress. And bedsheets and . . . oh. When his eyes opened fully, he saw he was in a hospital. Hovering over him like an asteroid about to crash into his face was Mom. He caught her expression just as it changed from genuine, tear-filled worry to "Just wait till we get home."

A nurse went to the window and pulled the drapes wide. The sun blasted through. CJ tried to raise his arm to shield his eyes, and that's when the pain shot through his whole upper body so fast and so sharp that he yelped. A cast enveloped his forearm.

"He wakes," the nurse said with a chirpy voice. Mom still had that stern look on her face and said nothing, so the nurse leaned over CJ and smiled and said, "You were out for a bit."

CJ's gaze darted nervously between Mom and the nurse. "Where's my board?" The only thing he could do without hurting was wriggle his fingers.

"Oooh, you're lucky that I ain't burn that thing in the backyard," Mom growled. "I oughta snap that thing in half. What did I tell you about getting on that thing? You have any idea how worried I was when I got the call that you were at the hospital? You lucky I *work* here so I could get here so fast, but oooh when we get back home, you're gonna wish you broke more than your arm, because I'm gonna—"

"Now, CJ, here's your medication," said the nurse, saving him from further berating. "You hit your head pretty hard." To Mom, "We're gonna keep him for a little longer just to make sure it's only a concussion and not anything more serious."

The sunlight was still too bright, but if CJ looked away from the window, he had to face Mom. He had to face the way she frowned at him, not just like he was in trouble and not just like she was disappointed in him. She looked scared.

So he turned back to the window and the sunlight so bright that he couldn't even see what outside looked like.

Pretty soon, Mom left to go back on her shift.

Taye stood in the doorway to the hospital room, skateboard tucked under her arm. Natural black hair combed out and relaxed so that it came down in one giant swoop over her right eye. Beat-up Converse All Stars, cargo pants, and a tank top—she dressed like the older skaters. The seventeen- and eighteen-year-olds who would stop by the skate park when they wanted some hometown training between competitions, the ones who had their own skate parks just like they had their own sponsors and their own crews and their own invites to skating competitions.

The nurse turned and let out a startled "Oh, hello!"

"Hi, Taye," CJ said in a sulky voice.

Taye leaned her board against the wall by the door, then came to CJ's side. "I *heard* you ate it bad," she said with a grin. "Heard it was epic."

The way she said it, with all that pride in her voice, made CJ grin. "I was trying a 540 McTwist."

Her eyebrows shot right up.

A voice by the door said, "You were trying a WHAT?!"

It was Haru. They rushed to CJ's bedside, almost shoving Taye aside. "Are you crazy? A 540 McTwist?"

"They *did* say you went upside down," Taye said.

CJ shrugged. "I dunno. I just . . ." Even without closing his eyes, he could see the vision—the same vision he got every time he let himself daydream. Him standing imperially at the top of the ramp with his board propped up on the lip, helmet loose on his head while fans held their phones up to watch his vert run at the Summer X Games. "CJ WALKER!" the announcer would boom over the crowd. Haru Murata. Taye Valentine. All of them with their names called before their events, all of them flying through the air or grinding along a rail, all of them looking way too cool as they effortlessly demolished the competition, Deadsy or Lostprophets playing in the background the whole time.

But everyone had grown quiet. Haru tapped Taye's shoulder and jerked their head to the doorway where Mom stood. She didn't have to open her mouth to let everyone know the party was over. They filed out with their heads bowed.

⬭ ⬭ ⬭

There was a TV in CJ's hospital room, but whether it was on or off, he didn't care. He'd gotten his phone back—cracked screen and all—and had his earbuds in. He'd had to go a whole day without it, but now balance was restored to the universe.

"Hi, I'm Tony Hawk, and welcome to Skate Support." CJ was so engrossed in the YouTube video, he didn't notice that the nurse had started unplugging things and messing with the bed. Mom stood by the door with his backpack, his board fitted into its slot between the straps.

"Let's go, Ceej," Mom said, snapping her fingers and waving CJ over to the changing area. "Get dressed."

"That's it? I can go?"

"Yes, they have to get your room ready for the next patient."

Other hospital personnel streamed into the room and began spraying disinfectant over all the surfaces, then wiping them down while others removed the curtains and replaced them with new ones. They looked like a race car crew in a pit station, buzzing with activity. And all the while, everyone was wearing a blue surgical mask over their face.

Everywhere was closed. In the week since he'd gotten home from the hospital, the parks, the school (there was talk of sending everyone iPads, but who would pay for that?), the church (Mom watched virtual sermons in bed), even the Guitar Center they used to hang out at had all shut down.

"It's the zombie apocalypse," Haru said over Face-Time.

"The skate park too?" CJ asked. A part of him hoped it'd still be open, that there'd at least be that place he could sneak out to, where he could train, even with a broken arm. If he could make it out there, maybe it wouldn't feel so much like his dream to one day compete at the X Games had been put on hold. But Haru shook their head.

"Look," they said, then sent a series of photos of the place roped off with police tape. It looked like a crime scene. "Everyone has to wear masks, and everyone's wiping down their tables and everything. The whole house smells like Clorox."

"This sucks." CJ needed to be outside. He'd been

cooped up indoors all week with nothing to do. No Netflix or PS4, because Mom had reduced her per diem hours at the hospital and so was always home watching the news. And she couldn't even tell him to check out books from the library and read because the library was closed too. "I almost wish it *was* the zombie apocalypse."

CJ was buried under his blankets when his phone screen lit up. It was Taye.

He slid the green call icon, and her face popped up. She was wearing a helmet. And she was moving.

No, she was *skating*.

"Yo," she said, breathless. She wore a face mask under her chin.

"Taye, what are you doing? I thought the stay-at-home orders . . ."

"I'ma be at your door in like two seconds."

It had been two and a half weeks since he'd been in the same room as someone who wasn't Mom.

CJ scrambled out of bed and almost tripped over a pile of clothes on his way out the room. He doubled back to put on his mask and the face shield Mom always insisted he wear, then came racing out just in time to see

Taye at the open front door doing that "I'm on my best behavior" smile she was so good at.

"Is CJ in?" she asked Mom, even though she knew very well that CJ was standing right in the hallway by the living room.

Mom looked CJ's way. "Right over there." She went to the kitchen and came back out with her lunch bag and her purse. At the door, she stepped into her hospital sneakers. "CJ, you know the rules. There's a curfew, and I don't need to tell you twice what happens I hear you been out tryna get arrested. The skate park is *closed,* you hear me?"

"Yes, Mom," CJ said from the hallway.

Mom nodded toward the fridge. "There's a rotisserie chicken in there for when y'all get hungry. Be safe now. And remember, SIX FEET." Then she was gone.

CJ let out a sigh. "What's up? I thought we were supposed to be indoors."

Taye went straight to the fridge and pulled out the chicken. She didn't even get any napkins or paper towels before opening it and tearing off a drumstick. "I'm so hungry," she said around a mouthful of cold chicken.

"What are you doing? I mean . . . what were you doing outside?" He made sure to keep his distance while she ate, squinting for any droplets he might see spraying from her mouth.

She swallowed a chunk of chicken CJ knew she hadn't chewed enough. "Deliveries."

" 'Deliveries'?"

She caught her breath, put her fist to her chest, then let out a soft burp. "Food bank downtown is doing food deliveries for folks that can't get to the supermarket. You know, folks that lost their jobs and can't buy their own groceries. Line's always around the block, but they make sure there's enough food to go out for people that put in requests early. That's what I been doing. Racing all over town."

CJ started to pluck at the chicken. "I can't."

"You can't deliver food to people in need? Your mom's not gonna be mad at you for literally being an angel. Besides, I already got Haru on board."

"They're gonna be there too?"

"We all need this, CJ. It's not training, but we're still getting some fresh air. Besides, you can't be going wild with that arm."

⁂

It was unreal following Taye around the city.

It wasn't like when they used to follow the older skaters to an abandoned pool, where they'd all spend the day trying out the same tricks over and over again. And it wasn't like in the skate park, where everything was arranged just right like in the video games. It wasn't even like Taye had turned the whole city into a skate park. It was something else. Seeing Taye skate like this, flowing down hills, swerving around corners, leaping over barriers, just getting from point A to point B, holding a bag of groceries half the time, it wasn't the type of thing made for cameras. It wasn't the type of thing you could get a ton of views for on TikTok. It was just skating.

And it was beautiful.

Haru's route often took them to a different part of the city than the neighborhoods CJ and Taye were sent to, but CJ was sure Haru felt the same thing CJ was starting to feel.

Always just a little bit behind Taye, he began to notice new things. He started perusing the ground for pebbles, seeing where the concrete was smooth and where it wasn't. Downtown was closed and quiet, but the walls and alleys and park paths turned into a second world. A world behind the one he already knew. When the only sound he could hear was the roll of his wheels on the ground, it was like the world went HD. Backroads he could wind down, vacant lots he could languidly carve through—everything was brighter, sharper. Because, he realized, he *had* to pay attention to it. All the stuff he used to just breeze by, he now had to notice.

As the sun was setting one night, the two of them

came down a park pathway that ended in a set of stairs. CJ swerved to a stop but Taye kept going without slowing down. He reached out a hand to stop her. She was heading straight for the stairwell. Best-case scenario: she'd bite it hard and lose the groceries she was carrying. Worst-case scenario: she'd wind up in the hospital. But before CJ could make a sound, there was the telltale clack of Taye's board launching into the air and he watched as she soared over the stairwell, her shirt whipping about her, the bag of groceries perfectly balanced against her chest, then she LANDED and smoothly swerved around the corner out of sight.

CJ must've been standing there with his mouth wide open for a whole two minutes, because she came skating back and shouted his name. "CJ. CJ!"

He snapped out of it.

"Come on, we gotta drop these off."

CJ considered the brown bag of groceries he'd pinned to his chest with his cast. Then he looked at that stairwell, suddenly the steepest stairwell he'd seen in his entire life. If anything, it looked like it was getting longer.

"CJ! Come on!"

He gulped. There was no way he was making that jump. He started backing away. Shame burned in the pit of his stomach. He had no problem flying upside down on a quarter-pipe. How could a simple set of stairs have him literally shaking in his sneakers? He shook his head, then kicked up his board and held it in the crook of his free arm as he slowly made his way down to the street.

CJ felt the weight of his bed shift. A hand patted his head softly. He pulled the blankets back to find Mom sitting there, still in her scrubs. Her whole body smelled like cleaning products, though, and there were lines on her face from her mask straps.

"Hey," she said softly.

He pulled the covers back over his head.

"Baby, what's wrong?"

She never talked like this, never in a voice this low or this soft. And she never asked how he was doing, not because she couldn't guess or she didn't already know. Not because her son was in any way ever a mystery to her. It was because she never needed to.

"Come on, CJ. Taye called. She's worried. And Haru says that you haven't talked to them in over a week."

Even if CJ wanted to talk to his mom, he didn't know where to start. How could he tell her that his hopes for spending the summer training were dashed? How could he tell her that he was starting to think he wasn't even that good to begin with? That a staircase had scared him like nothing had before? A simple asphalt staircase. Watching Taye fly over it was like watching your friend suddenly sprout wings. One moment, she was right next to you and you were keeping pace, then suddenly she was up at a level you'd never reach, leaving you behind. How could he explain to his mom that what he wanted more than anything—to hear his name cheered at a skate competition—was never going to happen all because of a wipeout and a stupid pandemic?

"I know it's a tough time right now," she said with a sigh. "Things are changing very fast. Things are getting canceled, things are shutting down. Nobody really knows what's happening. And . . . and it's getting pretty scary at work."

At that, CJ looked up and saw his mom doing her best to keep a happy face on. "Is it . . . is it dangerous?"

For a second, Mom didn't say anything. Then she nodded. "Yeah. Yeah, it's dangerous. But I'm safe. The hospital is doing everything it can to make sure we're safe. And there are a lot of brave people there right now saving lives." She rubbed his back. "Taye and Haru told me you were helping them out over at the food bank."

CJ nodded. "Do you get scared?" he asked.

"Of course I do." She laughed. "I should be asking *you* that question, all those skateboarding tricks you're always doing." A pause. "Well, do you?"

He sat up in bed and nodded.

"If you're scared, then why do you do it?"

He shrugged, ready to not answer, but then he started thinking about it. And he remembered.

He remembered the first time he stepped on a board—his own board. It was at the top of a slope, and he'd had no backup plan. He remembered pushing off. He remembered the instant acceleration. He remembered moving faster than he'd ever run. He remembered how he'd made the biggest of rookie mistakes. Instead of bending at the knees and spreading his arms wide, he'd locked his knees and stood up. The board rocked from side to side, left, then right. He remembered bailing right before the end of the slope and trying to run it out but then pitching forward and hitting the ground. Palms, chest, chin, his legs high up in the air behind him. Skidding until he got himself stuck under a car, jammed between the wheels and the curb. He remembered his legs poking out behind him, squirming, and thinking that he must've looked like a cartoon to Taye and Haru.

His first real wipeout. The first time he met a curb. The first time he noticed the steel edges—the coping—that would make it easier to grind on.

The first time he went that fast, he didn't care whether or not other people were watching or chanting his name. All that mattered was the board beneath him and the city speeding by around him.

"I was flying," he said to Mom when he came out of the memory. "And . . ." He looked at his hands, remembered how dirty and cut they were and how new it all felt. "Taye and Haru, they were there to pick me up after. I . . . I wasn't alone. Even if I went skating by myself, I wasn't alone. Not really." The joy of moving that fast—for no one but yourself—it was impossible to describe. But the look in Mom's eyes told CJ that, somehow, she understood.

She smirked and rubbed CJ's knee.

"You're not mad that I use my skateboard for deliveries?"

"Ain't no way I'm letting you use the van." She chuckled. "Ceej, it's okay to be scared. School, the world, all of it. But sometimes the best way to get past that fear is to get past yourself. Be of service to others." She winked. "Do a good deed and don't get caught."

CJ didn't realize he was about to cry until he sniffled up a wad of snot. Mom brought him into a massive hug. It felt good. It felt like he was getting something out of his system. Because now he wanted nothing more than to be in motion again.

CJ waved at the last family on the block after he dropped off their groceries, then turned to go. Even though everyone was wearing masks, he now knew when someone was smiling. Skateboard tucked under his arm, he caught up to Haru and Taye, who were finishing their rounds a few houses down.

In one smooth motion, he dropped the board while running and stepped onto it. Soon all three of them were gliding around the corner of the block and out onto the main street.

They were done for the night and had clocked out at the food bank, so all that remained was for them to split up and head home. There was a little time before curfew to skate on their own. To crash into walls while trying to figure out a wallride. To push up a hill, look down at your domain from its crest, then cut through the air like an arrow loosed from a bow, no cars on the road, no one yelling at you to watch out. To grind on a curb, board kissing the coping the only sound on the block.

CJ knew Taye and Haru did the same thing on their way home. It was how they stayed with each other, even without talking. So that when he finally got through the park to the top of the stairwell and the sun was setting and no one was there to watch him try what he was going to try, he knew he was not alone.

THE GENDER REVEAL

BY GEORGE M. JOHNSON

"Malcolm. You are gonna be late for the bus if you don't get a move on!" yelled the voice from the other room.

"Five more minutes, Mommy. Please?" yelled back Malcolm.

"Okay! Five minutes, and then you gotta get out the door."

Malcolm breathed a small sigh of relief and focused on putting a few more stitches in the outfit he had been working on over the last few days. Next to the sewing machine there was a sketch. A suit with a beautiful floral pattern sketched by Malcolm. A single button jacket with a Monk collar and tapered pants that stopped right at the ankle. It was stylish . . . but it wasn't quite what he wanted. Malcolm looked at the sketch and shrugged, saying under his breath, "Close enough."

As Malcolm pushed his foot down on the pedal, the sewing machine began stitching a seam along the pants line running smooth between his fingers. Malcolm was at his happiest when it was just him and his sewing machine, working on whatever newest creation he could come up with. But sometimes it felt like his designs were too much—too much for his friends, maybe, and *definitely* too much for his father, whom he adored. Hence the suit. (Even though it still had some of his signature flair.)

While he finished his stitches, he glanced up at the picture on the wall, the one of him sitting in his grandmother's lap. He was about five years old in the photo, and Big Nanny was teaching him how to use the sewing machine for the first time. Malcolm had a smile from ear to ear.

It was the same grin he wore in the original sketch he had drawn of his birthday outfit—the sketch that now lay buried beneath the pile of cloth scraps. The outfit in the sketch used the same purple and red floral pattern on top of a black fabric as the suit he was sewing now. But this sketch depicted a long, flowing train attached right at the waist. It was gorgeous and glamorous. But Malcolm just wasn't sure if he was ready to take that leap. So he shoved the old sketch out of his mind and focused on his suit.

"Okay, Malcolm, let's get a move on!" yelled his mother again.

"Coming!"

Malcolm grabbed his book bag off the floor and

walked out of the sewing room. He peeked into the kitchen, where his mother stood ironing his father's shirt and his little brother, Joshua, sat at the table eating a bowl of cereal.

"See you later," Malcolm said, to which his mom responded, "Okay, baby. Don't forget to make the list of songs you want your uncle Frank to play tomorrow!!!"

Uncle Frank was always at the DJ booth at their family gatherings. Malcolm gave his mom a thumbs-up.

Big Nanny was sitting in the living room as he passed through. Malcolm paused. "Big Nanny, can you do me a favor?"

"What you need, honey?"

"I didn't finish putting together the seam for the pants I'm making for my birthday outfit. Can you finish it up for me so I can put the last touches on the jacket after school?"

Big Nanny looked at Malcolm and smiled. "Of course. But you gotta give me some sugah before you go."

Malcolm walked over to her and kissed her on the cheek. Then he headed out the door toward the bus stop.

As Malcolm walked, the cool crisp air of autumn hit him in the face. Leaves were starting to turn that pretty orange color like they do when the seasons begin to change in New Jersey. With every leaf pile, Malcolm took a big jump, crunching down on the twigs and fallen leaves. Maybe it was a little babyish, but so what? That walk to the bus was five minutes of heaven.

Malcolm finally reached the corner. While he waited for the bus, he couldn't stop thinking about his birthday party the next day. He began singing Stevie Wonder's "Happy Birthday" under his breath.

Finally he saw the bus coming up the street. He walked up to the curb as the bus pulled up. "Good morning, MJ," said the bus driver as she opened the door, to which he responded, "Good morning, Mrs. Baker."

"Tell your nanny I'mma drop off that money when I get off tonight," she said with a smile.

Malcolm chuckled. "Okay, Mrs. Baker, I'll let her know." Big Nanny was always letting someone hold a few dollars—with interest, of course.

He walked six rows back and took his normal seat next to his bestie, Janet Jacobs, who was grinning up at him like usual. Janet was about five feet tall with a milk chocolate complexion. She was wearing a maroon sweater and a gray skirt with pleats, the regular uniform most of the girls wore. Today, her hair was back in a ponytail, and she wore a small strand of pearls around her neck. Malcolm and Janet had been best friends since kindergarten, and now that they were in their final year at Tubman Junior High School, they were tighter than ever.

"Hey, Janet, what's the tea?"

"Ain't nothing. Ready to get this Friday done with so we can party tomorrow. Are you excited?"

Malcolm nodded. "I'm a little behind on my outfit, but I should have enough time to get it done. Big Nanny is gonna work on the pants today so I can focus on the top."

"Well, that's good. You know she could sew a dress blindfolded. I know you gonna show out." Then Janet turned her head and narrowed her eyes at Malcolm. "Soooooo . . . have you decided if you are gonna go through with it?"

Malcolm took a deep breath in, then sighed and put his head down. "I decided to change the design to a regular suit. I don't think I'm ready to push my fashion that far in front of my dad."

Janet leaned in closer. "That's not the 'it' I'm referring to and you know it."

Malcolm lifted his head up and looked at Janet in her piercing eyes. "Oh. *That* 'it.'" He sighed. "I'm not sure if I'm ready to tell them I'm nonbinary. My dad isn't very big on words, you know."

Janet grabbed Malcolm's hand and held it tight.

"Yeah, your father is a bit on the tough side. But you know he loves you."

"Yeah, he definitely does." Malcolm felt his chest loosen up just a little bit. "Thanks, J."

"Always," said Janet. Then she muttered under her breath, "And your daddy is fine."

"Girl, bye!" Malcolm yelped. They both laughed.

Back at the house, Big Nanny slurped the rest of her breakfast and headed for the sewing room to finish up the pants for Malcolm's birthday outfit. As she sat down at the sewing desk, she reached for a spool of thread sitting on the edge of the table and accidentally knocked over the pile of scraps the thread had been sitting on. "Darn it," she said as she bent over to pick them up.

"What is this here?" she exclaimed out loud as she grabbed hold of a loose paper that had floated to the floor.

It was a sketch of Malcolm grinning in a glamorous design. Not the sketch of the suit—this one had a long, flowing train. The words at the top read "My Birthday Outfit."

Big Nanny looked at the pants on the table. Then she

looked at the jacket hanging in the closet. She took one last look at the sketch.

Big Nanny walked over to the closet and grabbed the jacket. She laid it out on the sewing desk and pulled out her scissors. With a grin on her face, she began cutting.

The school day was like any other day—switching classes, catching up with Janet in between periods, and running into class before the door closed. Malcolm couldn't pay much attention that day, though, knowing he had a birthday party coming up *and* a big decision to make. He just kept staring at the clock as it went from 1 p.m., to 1:30 p.m., to 2 p.m., and finally to 2:27 p.m. when the final bell rang.

Malcolm walked out of his last period class and met Janet at the lockers.

"You make a decision yet, boo?" Janet asked. Malcolm glanced at her with a side-eye.

"You are worse than my little brother when he want candy. I think I'mma just sleep on it and decide in the morning." Malcolm bit his lip. "I'm still so nervous about my birthday party outfit, though. I hope it doesn't underwhelm. Everyone looks to me for fashions, you know."

"Listen," Janet said, "you were best dressed in elementary school. You're going to be best dressed at the end of this year. Probably best dressed in high school and at the Emmys one day. The only thing now is if you are best dressed as a 'he' or a 'they.'"

Malcolm snapped his head back. "You don't ever give up, do you?"

"Nope. But for real, I've known you since you were five playing with my dolls and doing hair. I know who you are. You know who you are. Tomorrow you will just be inviting everyone else into that—if you want to, I mean. And I'll be right there by your side, wearing a cute dress and hoping Jimmy notices."

Malcolm pulled a face. "Girl, go away from me. Just boy crazy."

"And what are you??" Janet replied. They both laughed.

"Well, whatever you decide, you know I got your back," Janet continued. "Now, come on, we're gonna be late for cross-country practice." They linked arms and headed to the locker rooms.

⬤ ◦

While Malcolm was getting changed, a few of his teammates came up to him. Jimmy, their star basketball player who stood six feet tall already at age thirteen, was dark skinned with a brush cut. Jimmy and Malcolm had known each other since elementary school. "Yo, Malcolm, you seemed off all day today," said Jimmy. "You all right?"

"Yeah, I'm good, y'all. Just thinking about my birthday tomorrow." He sighed. "I have this thing I want to get off my chest, but I don't know if it's the right moment."

"I mean, what you thinking about?" Paul jumped in. Paul was Jimmy's sidekick. Good enough to make the teams, but definitely not the star. (Malcolm could relate.) He had a caramel skin complexion, and he was constantly lifting weights. "You already told us you were gay years ago. Wait, you dating girls now???"

"Shut up, Paul, you don't ever know what to say," Jimmy said.

"Look, Malcolm," Paul continued, "we all been knowing each other a few years now. At first when you came out, we was all nervous. But you mad cool. Just don't think too hard on whatever it is. We just want you to be yourself, bro."

Malcolm grinned. "Thanks, I appreciate that."

"Now get out on the track before Coach make us run extra laps," Paul joked. Malcolm winced and hurried to get dressed, then walked out with the team.

After practice, Malcolm and Janet headed to the front of the school to wait for his mom to come get them. To Malcolm's surprise, there was someone there who had never come to pick him up before.

"Daddy! What are you doing here?"

"Hey, boy," said Malcolm's dad, standing there in his sanitation supervisor jumpsuit. "I figured I'd take you and Janet for some pizza. A little prebirthday treat."

Malcolm's jaw dropped. His dad was always working or busy. But Malcolm wasn't about to pass up this opportunity. Malcolm and Janet jumped into his truck, and they all headed to Bruno's, the pizza shop in their town. Once they were seated, they ordered a giant pepperoni pizza.

"So, you excited about tomorrow?" asked his father.

"Yeah," Malcolm said, even as the nerves kicked up in his belly all over again. "I'm finally gonna be a teenager."

"And it's about time," Janet cut in. "You and this birthday later in the year is mad aggy."

"So what are you wearing?" Malcolm's father asked. "I know you, and I'm sure it's going to be something . . . different."

Malcolm's dad wasn't always the best with words,

so when he said "different," Malcolm knew what he meant. *Over-the-top. Colorful. Flamboyant.* Malcolm sighed. "Yeah, Daddy, it will be something different. Big Nanny is working on it with me."

Malcolm's dad smiled. "Big Nanny is always up to something with you. That's good, though."

Once they finished up their pizza, they all got back in the truck, and Malcolm's dad dropped off Janet at home. "We'll see you tomorrow, right?" Malcolm's dad asked.

"You know it, Mr. Jennings!" Janet exclaimed.

As soon as Janet walked into her house, Malcolm got a text from her. *Your daddy is still fine lol. Try to talk to him though.*

Malcolm responded with the rolling-eye emoji. *Okay I will.*

But the rest of the ride home was silent. Malcolm just couldn't get the words out his mouth. Once they got home, Malcolm rushed inside and went to his room to do his homework. He moved so fast that he didn't even get a chance to speak to Big Nanny or his mother. He just went in his room, slammed the door, and buried his head in his books.

Malcolm felt the weight of the world was on his chest. He always felt like what he wanted to say was right on the tip of his tongue, but he could never just let it all the way out. And yeah, he had felt supported after naming his sexuality, but this was different. This was heavier. And he didn't know how all of them—his friends, his family, his father—would take it.

Malcolm spent three hours in his room working on homework. But he really wasn't working on it. He was rereading passages over and over. Just stuck in his head contemplating what to do. Malcolm finally got up and went into the sewing room to talk to Big Nanny. But when he opened the door and saw what was hanging on the rack, he gasped.

The two-piece design Malcolm had started was no more. The jacket was now attached to the pants, making it a one-piece outfit, and at the hips of the outfit there now was a long, flowing train attached. Through the opening in the front, the floral pattern of purple and red shimmered against the gorgeous black fabric.

"This is so beautiful, Big Nanny," he said.

But Malcolm still felt his nerves creeping in. He looked over at Big Nanny.

"I can't wear this, Big Nanny. I'm not ready for it."

Big Nanny gave him a look. "Ready for what, Malcolm? I know you, baby. *We* know you. It's okay. You can say it to me."

Malcolm's eyes filled up with tears. He wanted to speak, but the words couldn't seem to escape his mouth.

Big Nanny patted the seat next to her. "Sit down, Malcolm, I wanna tell you a story." She took a deep breath and went on. "Your uncle Frank isn't really your dad's brother."

Malcolm's eyes got big as quarters at that. "What??"

"When your dad was fifteen, he and Frank were best friends. Back during that time, Frank was what you would refer to as 'soft.' I think the word they used back then was 'sissy.' Well, one day, Frank's father found out that he was gay. He hurt Frank pretty badly. Your dad always knew about Frank but never cared. So when Frank came to him, your dad brought him back to the house and asked if Frank could stay with us. Of course I took him in without a second thought, and the two have remained best friends ever since."

Malcolm looked up at Big Nanny in awe. "I never knew that about Daddy. He just always seems so closed off. Like, I know he loves me, but it just isn't his easiest emotion to show."

"I know, baby. But one thing I do know is that your father is one of the most caring and understanding people on this earth. And that you shouldn't be afraid to tell him your truth. 'Cause if he even tries to reject you, I'll knock him out."

Malcolm sat up and laughed. "Thanks, Big Nanny."

She pulled Malcolm in for a tight hug. "Okay, now let's practice."

Malcolm gave her a sharp look. "Uh, practice what?"

"Your truth. Go ahead and stand right there and say what you've always wanted to say!"

Malcolm wanted to say that he couldn't. That it was too much. But then he drew himself up and stood tall in front of Big Nanny. He grabbed the outfit off the hanger and walked behind the dressing wall they had in the room. Once he'd tried it on, he came from around the corner and saw it for the first time in the mirror. He couldn't keep the smile from tugging at his cheeks. The outfit needed a few alterations but it was perfect. He felt powerful, like a superhero when they put on their cape.

Malcolm turned and let Big Nanny take a look at him. Then he took in a deep breath and finally said the words:

"Big Nanny. I am nonbinary. My pronouns are no longer 'he' and 'him.' I would like to be referred to as 'they' and 'them.'"

"Well, all right! Seems to me like you got it down. Now you gonna have to explain to me what non . . . that word you said fully means, but I think I get what you're putting down!"

Malcolm let out a big exhale. "Thanks, Big Nanny."

Big Nanny just smiled and nodded.

"All right, we need to get ready for tomorrow, now. Go and get you some rest."

Malcolm smiled. Leaned in and gave her a kiss on the cheek. Then they walked into their room, climbed up to the top bunk bed, and clapped twice for the lights to go out. Their little brother, Joshua, was already asleep. Malcolm took a deep breath and closed their eyes.

It was finally the big day. Malcolm had butterflies running through their stomach. They took a shower, ate breakfast, and relaxed a little bit. The party didn't start until noon, so they had some time to get their thoughts together. But before Malcolm knew it, it was eleven o'clock.

Big Nanny peeked out of the sewing room and saw Malcolm sitting in the living. Malcolm looked over to her and grinned. Big Nanny grinned right back. "Time to get dressed!"

Malcolm stood on a little footstool that Big Nanny's mother had made many years ago. You couldn't see the stool, though, because it was all being covered by the train that extended out about seven feet from Malcolm's waist. A beautiful floral print jumpsuit with the floral print train to match. Malcolm had on their superhero cape again. The outfit gave them the powers of truth.

Malcolm looked back over their shoulder. "I think I'm ready, Big Nanny."

Big Nanny winked. "Let's do this."

Malcolm came down off the footstool and began walking toward the door. Big Nanny grabbed the train to make sure it wasn't dragging on the floor. Malcolm walked through the house toward the back door, where everyone was awaiting them outside.

Big Nanny exited first. Malcolm looked out the window to see everyone out there—Janet, their friends, their family, even Uncle Frank warming up the crowd with some Jersey club music. A lump formed in Malcolm's throat and their hands got clammy. Malcolm rubbed their sweaty hands on the train. Then they grabbed the train and looked back at it trailing behind. Malcolm took another breath and knew they were ready.

"May I have your attention, please," Big Nanny said, clapping her hands to get the crowd to quiet down. "My grandbaby Malcolm has something to tell all of you. I would like for you all to gather around and allow Malcolm the space to say what needs to be said."

Everyone looked around in confusion. Malcolm's parents looked at one another and took a sip of their drinks.

Malcolm watched them all nervously. Then they took a deep breath and stepped out the door, the train flowing out behind them.

The audience gasped. Malcolm looked at Janet, their nerves taking over. Janet yelled, "You got this, Malcolm! And I got you." Malcolm's lips quirked up in a tiny smile.

No more fear, they whispered under their breath. The lump in their throat began to ease. Malcolm released the sides of the train and took another deep breath in. Then they smiled and began speaking.

"My name is Malcolm Jamal Jennings. Today I am thirteen years old. I am nonbinary. My pronouns going forward are 'they' and 'them.'"

As soon as Malcolm finished speaking, everyone was silent, including both of Malcolm's parents. Malcolm's eyes started filling with tears, their hands back on the train, bunching in the fabric. Malcolm wanted to turn and run back into the house, but before they could make that dramatic exit, they heard a familiar voice. "And we love you, baby!" yelled Big Nanny. Malcolm looked at her and could see love and pride in her eyes.

And then it happened.

Malcolm's father started clapping. Then their mother. Then everyone else. Malcolm smiled in disbelief as a tear rolled down their face.

Malcolm's father walked up to them and gave them a hug. "I'm really proud of you, Malcolm." Malcolm buried their head in their father's chest. Malcolm's mother came up and hugged them both. Then Malcolm's parents stepped away to make room for Malcolm's friends, who were crowding around them.

"Malcolm, you always got something going on," Paul said. "But that's what's up. Wish more folks could be as brave as you." They both dapped each other up. Jimmy walked up with a plate of food, and Janet immediately ran over with a napkin for him. Malcolm looked at Janet and muttered, "So thirsty."

Then Jimmy said, "Malcolm, you never cease to amaze me. Mad respect. Just don't wear that to cross-country practice." Malcolm laughed and dapped him up too.

Uncle Frank was clapping just as loud behind the DJ booth. He started playing music and then got on the mic. "All right, all right, I wanna give a shout-out to my nibling, Malcolm!" Malcolm looked at Uncle Frank. "Hey, I been in this community awhile. I know the lingo."

Janet whooped and started dancing. Malcolm joined in too, swirling their train in a circle as the air caught underneath it. Malcolm and Janet began two-stepping with one another to the beat. Malcolm smiled hard as they rocked their body from side to side.

Everyone else at the party moved toward the dance floor, and Big Nanny even got in the middle while everyone clapped. Then Malcolm's dad, followed by their mother and their little brother. After a beat, Big Nanny smirked and gestured for Malcolm to join her in the center. Malcolm just smiled and laughed as they danced their way toward her and the rest of the family, holding their train like they were in a fairy tale and feeling lighter than air.

KASSIUS'S FOOLPROOF GUIDE TO LOSING THE TURKEY BOWL

BY DAVAUN SANDERS

Three minutes before halftime is over. I pluck at my kente bow tie for the hundredth time. Pretend like my dress shirt isn't stuck to my back. Wipe my forehead. Check the cake—our backyard trees shade the canopy, but the buttercream frosting is sweating worse than I am. My question is written in fancy cherry-red cursive that the cake lady promised me is undefeated. Except Maya's not here to answer—another few minutes and she won't even be able to read it.

I smell amazing, at least. I think.

Two minutes. My team's gonna be looking for me soon. I unfold a flickering silver hole in the air. My Fuerza is portals, and I can will them open to anyplace I've tried so far. Legend stuff, right? But this portal's just peeking back at the street in front of our house. Game's about to start. This has got to work. I close my portal, clap two times, and yell out: *"Ball!"*

Maya heard that. Had to. I try not to twirl the rose stem between my fingers. Footsteps. Finally. She's *here,* this is my time to *shine*. I turn and—it's just Daed, ducking into the canopy.

"We are *late,* bro!" He winces at the table. "Dang. She didn't find the cake?"

"The frosting is kinda melty. It's supposed to say 'no' on the left corner and 'yes' on the right. Can you read it?"

"Yeah, but—is that supposed to be you and Maya?"

"Yeah . . ."

He squints. "I like the red jacket, but they got your skin a little . . . green."

"She loves 'Thriller,' okay? I don't make the rules."

"Whatever. Can we please go win this—" Daed stops and sniffs. "Wait. What's that smell?"

"A lil bit of Pop's Faux-Bama."

"Kash!"

"What? It's a big day up in here!"

"My guy, you don't put on cologne over sweat. That's fresh funk!"

"Whatever. It's going to work. I'm telling you! We only gotta see it through."

"Just . . . get your head in the game, okay? I got Auntie Deidra to make my boo try her jalapeño mac and cheese. You know he hates playing defense with the bubble guts." He cuffs my shoulder and gives me a look. "But I need my running back."

I reluctantly set the rose down beside the cake. I shed the formal gear and pull on my custom-made jersey with our team name, Cheat Code Squad. Turkey Bowl official. Gold and scarlet—my pop's shout-out to the best team to ever do it. Rocking number 21 like my fave running back.

We hustle out to Vancey Street. Our whole cul-de-sac is shut down for First Peoples' Remembrance Day, cars stuffed into garages or moved around the corner for the big game. The Jacksons' yard is full of kinfolk going in on third and fourth plates from long tables stacked with turkey, corn bread, all manner of salads, stuffing, ham, mashed potatoes, grilled tofu, greens, cranberry sauce, mac and cheese, and roasted veggies. And don't even get me started about desserts.

These are our people, all with some kind of Fuerza, speedsters and energy conductors rubbing elbows with shape-shifters, matter manipulators, and more. And that's only the stuff they've figured out names for.

Chairs fill the entire yard and some folks even perch on surrounding rooftops. Team Glitch is huddled up already with Royce, Daed's boyfriend, serving up their attack plans. He rubs his belly and I grin—that jalapeño mac must be getting to him.

My heart does a little wiggle at the sight of Maya, pushing a pebble down the gutter with one of her

Chucks. She's pulled up her hoodie, but I stray close enough to catch a hint of jojoba from her freshly twisted locs. Maya's Fuerza, time travel, is rare—I think it's why she likes old stuff—but she'd still be amazing without it.

I smile. "Every year, sitting on the curb. Are we ever gonna get you to play?"

"Play? Time travel and football fit together like . . . I don't know . . ."

"Jalapeños and mac and cheese?" I offer.

Maya's lips twitch. "I'm lucky they still let me referee." She thumbs back at her folks, who are suddenly hawking me from across the greens pot.

"We good, Maya?"

"Fine, Mom!" She sighs and begins scrolling her phone. "You better go. Last time I got in trouble, they made me spend a weekend living two hundred years ago. No Wi-Fi." She shudders. "And we churned actual butter."

A huge arm lassoes my shoulders. "Kassius. Would you leave that girl be?" Pop finally stopped dyeing the gray in his goatee, but he's just as strong as his superhero days. Pop coaches Cheat Code Squad along with Daed's dad. His nose wrinkles, and he sniffs the air around me. "Why does it smell like Leader of the Free World's armpit around here?"

I shrug off his arm. "They, uh . . . need me in the huddle!"

"Please go win this one!" he hollers after me. "I don't need to hear Royce's old man flapping his gums about this game all the way to Kwanzaa!"

Daed gives me a pressed look as I finally join Cheat Code Squad's huddle. I glance around at our other teammates: Syd warps gravity, and Valencia is an elemental. He's a little scary, and she might weigh a buck soaking wet, but Daed—our QB—couldn't ask for better line protection. "We gotta slow down the summoning or they finna cook us like last year. Vonchi, you want some getback, right?"

"You know this!" Our wide receiver Vonchi's palms glow in anticipation. "Just throw me the ball."

"Run straight at him. Kash will be on time." Daed flashes me a look. "Right?"

A voice shivers into my brain. *You know this plan of yours is busted.*

"Laurence, go on somewhere!" I shout as I peek over at Team Glitch's huddle. Laurence, their skinny telepath, smirks and waves. Great. Royce must have filled them in on my plan, because they all look big mad.

"Told you," Daed hisses. "No one messes with Turkey Bowl, not for nothing!"

"We good," I say hastily. "I got you, Vonch!"

Daed snorts, levitating the football over his palm as we line up. Turkey Bowl rules are simple: sidewalk is out of bounds. Four quarters with four downs, four chances to score a touchdown. Our Fuerza is part of the game. I'm wide right, and Vonchi is to the left. Our kinfolk still in anticipation on the sidelines, murmuring and nudging each other in the ribs, sliding their sunglasses on.

"Blue, one-zero! *Kwanzaa!*" Daed claps twice, glares at me—then does a quick spin, crisp as a ballerina. Perfect! Chortles erupt from the seats, but Maya's scrolling her phone. She missed it!

"What's with the dancing?" Daed's dad barks. "Play ball!"

"Blue, one-zero! Go!"

Vonchi and I both streak down the street. My defender gives me plenty of cushion, instead of jamming me at the line with their dark matter powers. Royce is Team Glitch's safety; he cheats over to help cover Vonchi. She's faster than everyone else on the street.

Daed heaves a perfect back-shoulder fade to her side. I raise a portal up right behind her, a translucent disk of mercury. She turns, snags the ball, vanishes through it—

—then pops out of its twin, five yards behind her defender. He tries to turn, but his ankles fold up! He plops on the asphalt as she tears up the street.

The crowd gives a thrilled scream. Royce barrels toward Vonchi. Light blazes from Vonchi's free palm at Royce, who flails back with a lightning strike. She staggers, and Laurence saves the touchdown with a shoestring tackle.

"Second down," Maya calls.

Next play is mine. We stayed up late after last night's spades tournament, working out the physics. "Green, fifty-*two*!" Daed slips on a single white glove, then claps his hands. Twice.

I shift and trot back toward him.

Maya's frowning at Daed. More importantly, at his glove. Yes! We finally got her attention.

"Motion!" Royce calls. "Watch the trick play from the ugly one!"

"Green, fifty-forget-you! Go!"

I take the direct snap from our center, Syd. Team Glitch's summoner blitzes with her Fuerza. The street ripples with motes of red light. Little creatures with red webbed feet pour out of the ground like giant slimy tadpoles! Syd scampers back with a shriek, but still centers his density warp on the football. At the same time, Daed's levitation vaults me forward.

My job? Don't. Drop. The. Rock.

I smash through the netherworld beasties like a bowling ball. But instead of sailing straight into the end zone,

I sink to the street. Syd's completely shook—beasties are gumming on his shoelaces and he's lost control of his Fuerza. I'm stuck! Fences angle toward the street. Trees creak and lean toward the football. Cracks spiral through the asphalt.

Royce drags himself forward to touch me. "Down!" he shouts. "Call 'em off!"

The battle guppies wriggle into the asphalt. Gravity goes back to normal and I take in a big gulp of air. Energy crackles around Royce as we stand up. "You need to focus and play ball," he warns. "Do you know how hot her folks will be if they figure out your plan?"

"Third down," Maya calls. Maybe Royce is right. I can't tell if any of this is working or not. She won't even look my way.

"Your boo is doing too much," I tell Daed, back in the huddle.

"He ain't the only one. Vonch, I'm looking for you again."

I bite my tongue. Daed's under extra pressure—his dad and Pop want this dub. Bad.

I line up closer to help him. If Team Glitch summons more beasties, I'll portal them into Royce's bedroom.

"Gold, twenty-two! Go!"

Vonchi races forward and cuts across the middle behind Royce. Her defender gets roasted once again—but Laurence backpedals to help. My defender rushes for Daed, snatching webs of glowing black tar from thin air. Daed vaults over the attack, ready to heave the ball—but Vonchi's defender is a shape-shifter: two of her wave for the pass.

I'm wide open. "Throw the ball to *me!*" I slap, slap my hands together, whip kick my leg out, and throw my own white-gloved hand up high. Sure, Maya's frowning, but that doesn't matter. She saw!

Daed checks down to me. I get ten yards with the ball before Royce's lightning snatches my quads. I lob a portal at the ground, blind—anywhere that keeps me from being called down by contact. I fall through the flash of silver. My arms and legs flail for an instant before I crash into freezing water.

What the—? Then I remember: last week's science project in the Pacific. Royce is still behind me, gurgling in frustration. His lightning won't work down here. I toss out another portal—

—and spill back onto Vancey Street. Water gushes through the hole in the air behind me. A touchdown is just ten yards away, but the end zone suddenly lurches off into the distance, like our block just grew a mile long. *No way you're gonna win this, fam!*

Is there anything worse than a telepath messing with your brain? "Laurence, get out of my head!"

"I got you, Kash!" Vonchi shouts. I squeeze my eyes shut an instant before her light pulses out. Laurence groans beside me, but still manages to grab hold of my jersey. Syd centers his gravity Fuerza on Laurence, who suddenly weighs twenty pounds. He gets the stiff arm and goes sailing into the Jacksons' fence.

The street snaps into focus with Laurence out of the way. The end zone's right there!

Electricity locks up my whole body. Royce springs out of nowhere, sopping wet, and absolutely trucks me. I slap into the asphalt so hard that windowpanes rattle up and down the street.

Royce's celebration would make Patrick Willis cry tears of pride. Ocean water pools in the crater around me. A few unlucky tuna flop around on the street. Vonchi glares at one like she's tempted to kick it.

"Come on now," my pop calls.

"Team Glitch for the dub! Who. Y'all. Messing. *With!*" Royce looks down at me, smiles, and claps two times. Then he throws up zombie arms and high-steps around me, left, then right, then left again.

"Sportsmanship!" my pop rumbles.

Royce hastily yanks me to my feet. "Thank you!" I whisper. "That was perfect!"

"You're a buster and I lost your stupid glove in the ocean," he whispers back. "Good luck!"

Maya frowns at us behind her sunglasses. "Fourth down coming up."

I limp back to the huddle, remembering to close my portal. Folks are carrying off huge bluefin tuna, laughing, calling loudly for coolers. Maya's dad is boiling water off the flooded street using his Fuerza—heat induction—and he's chuckling too.

Daed gazes at the end zone and sighs. We're right there. We can score. But if we do, Maya won't have a reason to time travel—and my whole plan is worthless. It's not fair to my team, but before I even ask, Vonchi claps a hand on my shoulder and says, "You owe us big, Kash!"

"I'll never forget this, y'all!"

Daed shakes his head, but a smile quirks his lips. "It's on you now—I hope you're right."

I limp over to where Pop and Daed's dad are nursing their lemonades. They're both cackling because the losing team's coach grills for the whole block. "Maybe we can teach him how to sear some tuna after he finishes up our ribs," Daed's dad wheezes.

"You aight?" Pop asks. "Royce laid one on you."

"Pop." I meet his gaze. "I need you to throw the challenge flag. I'm pretty sure they've been . . . cheating."

Both men stop smiling. "Say what now?"

I tap my temple. "Laurence was in our huddle back at the beginning."

Even if you get grounded over this, Laurence whispers in my head, *I'mma still need all your comic books. Hand delivered.*

Bet, I think back at him. *That's the deal.*

"Son," Pop says warningly. "Calling folks cheaters? That's not how we do."

"Pop, I need this one. Please."

They exchange a long look. "You been playing at something all day."

"All week," I admit.

"If this is about . . ." Pop glances at Maya, then takes a long pull from his lemonade and sighs. "I was shole looking forward to those ribs."

He plucks a red bandanna from the belt loop of his jeans, the gravel inside it tied around with a rubber band to give it a little weight. He flings it. Disbelieving gasps ripple through our friends and family as the challenge flag lands in the middle of the street.

Maya stands straight up. She strides up to us and peels off her sunglasses. "A challenge? For what?"

Pop flashes me a sideways frown. "It's on you."

"Cheating." Her eyebrows rise as I continue. "Laurence spied on our plays. We tried to call it out, so you could find it faster when you time travel back. Like this."

I clap two times.

"Those are all the ones we need you to review, all right?" I catch Maya's eyes, and she searches my face. "You better . . . go."

And I clap two times again.

Maya gives her head a little shake. Light bursts around me like shattered stained glass as she winks into the past.

Six words. That's it. That's all I need her to find.

Daed clasps my shoulders. "Still think it worked?"

Maya winks back and Daed hops aside with a yelp. "Now I know you lying," she growls. "Daed's boo clapped before his stupid dance. Why would Royce snitch on his own team?"

I give an innocent shrug. "*So* weird. Did he say anything?"

She blinks, then flashes away and back. "'With'? Make it make sense, bruh!"

"It will, I promise. But there's more for you to check out first."

She gives me a look, then she's gone again.

"You almost blew it," Daed fusses at Royce. "Those moves? Trash."

"Whatever! I worked hard on that zombie dance. Besides, she saw it and remembered my word. What's next, Kash?"

Before I can answer, Maya winks back with a mystified scowl. " 'Me'? What kind of joke is this?"

I offer an innocent shrug. "Only one way to find out . . . !"

She winks off again.

Three words left. I catch my breath.

"My parts are next," Daed is saying. "The white glove? Clutch."

"But he didn't even wear it in 'Thriller,' " Royce protests, holding his stomach. Oh. Right. Jalapeños.

"I should've worn the glove," Vonchi puts in. "She wouldn't have missed that."

Maya winks back. My heart starts beating again. " 'Two.' 'Kwanzaa'?" she asks.

Maya's brown eyes meet mine, and she disappears in a flash of Fuerza. It's beautiful and confusing, a rainbow caught in a spin cycle. If my plan holds, she'll find her way to my backyard, the canopy, and the cake. Back where this all started, and where it ends.

"My guy." Daed nudges me. "You still really think this worked?"

Can't answer. Too busy holding my breath. I know this worked. It had to work. Please work. Time travel makes my head hurt if I think on it too long. But we ain't called Cheat Code Squad for nothing. I like Maya, and I'm mostly, pretty sure she likes me back.

Maya winks back—but no. There's no cake! No corner slice! My big plan didn't work. And I'm starting to feel real sick.

"This was a whole mess, Kash," she says.

"Yeah." Disappointment curdles in my chest, but I mumble my way around it. "I probably got us both in trouble." I risk a glance at our folks, who are grumbling from the sidewalk, before my gaze slides back down to the street. Okay, definitely in trouble. "Sorry."

"Was it worth it?" Something in Maya's voice makes me look back up.

She's holding my rose.

Our friends all gather in close, cheesing hard. Daed and Royce gesture at me furiously, and I realize I haven't said anything back to her yet.

"Yeah—er, no—yes!" *Geez!* What are words right now? "I mean: Yes. It was worth it."

Maya twirls the rose stem in her fingers. "So I guess you want an answer, huh?"

"Please!" Royce groans.

"Put this boy out his misery," Vonchi adds.

She shakes her head, disappears, only to return with the cake. The buttercream isn't melted as bad as

I thought. There's Maya and me with our red jackets, greenish skin, and matching white gloves. Thriller zombies in kente suits dance in formation behind us. I can still read the words in undefeated cherry-red script:

GO WITH ME a KWANZAA BALL!

Vonchi pulls out a phone to record. Royce and Daed hold the cake. Pop's eyes are full of love and dap and pride. And Maya's dad doesn't boil me out of my jersey.

I *knew* this would work out!

Maya leans in so close that her whisper tickles the baby hairs on my neck. "You get points for my zombie cake, bruh. But this looks like buttercream. I hate butter, Kash." She grabs a corner of cake and smears it across my face. My friends all howl and rain jokes that will live on forever in video; our parents dab their eyes and smile. But I don't care about the clowning, losing the Turkey Bowl, or even getting in trouble . . .

Because Maya grabbed the right corner, the one that says "yes."

BUT ALSO, JAZZ

BY JULIAN RANDALL

After the service wraps up, my older cousin, Brandon, loosens his tie and comes over to me. Suits don't really look right on him, even if he's prolly done growing at seventeen. Brandon's tall and wiry with a head full of waves, and looks way more at home in a black Champs hoodie than he ever does with a suit billowing around him. Grief don't fit all the way right on anybody, at least not today.

This morning's service was for Tre, who was two grades above me. I didn't know him well, but he used to make beats for Brandon sometimes, plus his mom and mine were in the same grade at Marshall Grove High. It's the fifth funeral since the start of June, three weeks ago. During Tre's service, we sang the same songs as we did for Bri after 12 got her last week, and Damon on the first day of June. Routine.

"Yo, Mikkel, you maintaining?" Brandon says in his fake-casual flow.

Maybe he's just keeping an eye on me. Nah, scratch that, I know that voice—something's up.

"Coolin, I just . . ." I trail off.

What is there to say I didn't say last week, or the week before? The whole congregation even seems at a loss for words. I look around, and all that's changed from last week is the photo. Nobody knows if this will be how the whole summer goes; no one wants to speak it into being. But we keep ending up here.

"It's okay not to be okay, Kel, you know that, right?" Brandon plops a palm on my shoulder. I'm grateful, but I shrug it off anyway.

"Yeah, no doubt," I say under my breath, scanning the congregation for my mom.

If everything's going according to routine, she finna pull up in a hot second and carpool me and Brandon and Aunty Toni back to our apartment building. We'll sit for a while in the main room of Aunty Toni's apartment, which smells like cinnamon and old newspapers and feels even more like home to me than our spot. We'll all sit and eat to-go plates from the block party and Aunty Toni and Momma will take turns saying "beautiful service," and me and Brandon will sneak away to his room to watch battle rap comps until it's time to go. The rest of the day, Momma will try to be supportive, but man, she be right up under me, following me from room to room like a really emotional Roomba.

But today Brandon's got a nervous look on his face. Brandon's never nervous. Something's up.

"Ma says that Pastor Sweat wants to see us in his office." Brandon strokes his waves with a small brush as he says it.

"Both of us? What did I do??" I try to keep the cold dread trickling down my back out of my voice, but it cracks into a weird squeak. Puberty really merciless out here.

"Aight, well, *technically* he just asked Moms for me, but like, y'know, come for moral support, cuzzo?"

"You buggin." I snort, earning a glare from a passing church elder. Everybody's a critic. "Look, Pastor Sweat cool and all, but I ain't even do nothing!"

"Dawg, neither did I . . . that he knows about . . . I think!" Brandon starts going even harder with the wave brush. "Just like, stay on my hip, you won't even have to say nothing. *Be in and out, no doubt?*"

Dang, he quoted the first rhyme I ever shared with him. Back when I was a lil homie and Brandon had first started rapping, I slid him my "hottest bars" to use. The thought of going onstage like Brandon makes me even more nervous than I am normally. But back when we were kids I loved watching him take the words I wrote and make them dance in a way my mouth never has been able to. They were all trash, but he told me to keep 'em coming, so I did. I think that's when he became my best friend. I'd say favorite cousin, but it's been just the two of us for as long as I can remember. If Brandon's desperate enough to quote my own rhymes, he must think Pastor Sweat extra hot at him for something. Now I gotta go with him—it's cousin law.

"Y'know, one of these days that's going to stop working," I say, crossing my arms.

"Is that day today?" Brandon straightens his tie.

"Nah, not today. But one day—"

"I'mma worry about one day when it's one day, then." Brandon laughs, and then more quietly: "Thanks, cuzzo. Let's go see what Pastor Sweat wants."

The important thing to know about Pastor Sweat is that his forehead be dry as a third grader's toothbrush. We just call him Pastor Sweat because he looks like Keith Sweat. And both our moms *love* Keith Sweat, so I'm kind of an expert, feel me?

Me and Brandon knock lightly on the door to Pastor Sweat's office and hear his deep voice rumbling through the door. Inside, the office is cramped and smells like rose-scented candles and thick church robes. Which makes sense, because besides a tiny desk with some balled-up papers on it, that's pretty much all that's in there. Pastor Sweat raises his eyebrows when he sees me along with Brandon but cracks a weary smile anyway and gestures at the two stackable chairs in front of his desk. His nameplate shines, the words REV. DOMINIC SHARP in clean metallic font like a discount grill.

"Hi, Pastor," Brandon says, voice a little tight. "Before we get to talkin, I just wanted to say I'm sorry."

"Sorry?" Pastor Sweat says, stroking the gray spot in his goatee. "But, Brandon, I—"

"It only *looked* like I was sleep last Sunday. Allergies, y'know? Anybody who say otherwise is, uh, bearing false witness!"

"Brandon, you're not in trouble for that. All I'm trying to—"

"And I never would've did anything to disrespect Tre, especially not at his homegoing," Brandon says in a rush. "He was my homie. I only started rapping because he gave me beats. I mean, he was the one who told me about decibels, and that's how I became—"

"Decibull," Pastor Sweat says, pinching the bridge of his nose as he says Brandon's rap name, but smiling at the same time. "I've seen your tapes from Sunday Sixteens, young brother—you've got the gift. No doubting that; you've been blessed. I'm counting on it, actually."

"Whatchutalmbout, Pastor?" Brandon tips his head to the side. I'm curious, too.

"Look, y'all, it's no secret that these have been some challenging weeks for the congregation. From where I'm standing, everyone's feeling a bit weary. So I have a request for you, Brandon. I'd like you to write a song for the congregation, and I'd like you to perform it at the church BBQ next Sunday. Think you could handle that?"

Both our jaws hang open. Did our pastor just ask for a rap song? Shouldn't he want . . . I don't know, smooth R and B? Jazz? What do grown-ups listen to when they feel like no one is listening?

"You listen to rap music?" I exclaim.

"You listen to *my* music?" Brandon says, slow, like he's tasting the words.

"Y'all gotta stop looking so surprised before I get offended!" Pastor Sweat grins. "You know I'm not *that* old, right? Now, about this song idea . . ."

"Hol up," I hear myself say. "You want, like . . ."

"Gospel rap?" Brandon finished.

"Not necessarily. More just, something to remind our flock that joy will come in the morning, feel me? I've seen your videos, Brandon, and you've got a way with the crowd. I want some of that lyricism to give us a shot in the arm. It's not a death sentence to be Black, but I think the way June's gone, sometimes we can forget."

I shoot a look at Brandon, who is nodding, a slight frown on his face, the waves on his head glistening in the thin beam of light from the window. Pastor Sweat isn't wrong. Since the summer started, I'd felt heavier and heavier. I'd look at Mr. Porter, from the building next door, or Brandon's beat-making homie, Prodigious, or Momma and Aunty Toni; between the police and all these funerals, it feels like we'll just keep getting heavier and heavier until the summer pulls us into the ground. Whatever might give folks a break from that has to be worth trying, and if anyone can do it, it's my big cousin.

Pastor Sweat stands up and leans on his desk.

"So, fellas, what do you say? Think you can help us out?"

Aunty Toni is the last one into our faded blue Taurus. "A song for the church?!" she booms the minute the door creaks shut. "Can you believe it? Oh, baby, I'm so proud of you. My son, making music for the community. Ain't that something?"

"Absolutely!" Momma says, catching Brandon's eye from the rearview mirror, the laugh lines near her eyes expanding and contracting like wings. "What do you think you'll do come Sunday, nephew?"

"Not sure yet, Titi," Brandon mumbles, thumbing his wave brush. "I'm sure it'll come to me tonight. It always does."

By the time we arrive back at Aunty Toni's apartment and open their peeling olive-green door, Mom and her are talking about the service again. I love how their apartment always has two cinnamon candles burning, how the candles drape the whole room in pinked light like a sunrise. We pick at our to-go plates for a while, and eventually Brandon excuses himself to his room to go work on the track for the church BBQ. I can't put my finger on it, but something is off with him. Then again, he looks normal enough on the outside, and his head is bobbing up and down like it does when he's getting ready to catch the beat at Sunday Sixteens at Duke's, the corner spot we all hang out at. I love kickin it with Brandon backstage, because everyone else always looks mad rattled by the crowd or the lights or the fear of not knowing what beat Duke is going to drop when it's their turn—but my cousin feeds off it. Just kicks it backstage, not talking to nobody, just bobbing his head and—

"His eyes," I mutter to myself.

"What you say, baby?" Aunty Toni says. "You want some more juice?"

"Oh." A wave of heat rolls up my face. "No thank you, ma'am. I was just thinking about a song."

"Y'know what, kiddo? Me too! I was just thinking, Willow, you remember that night back in '89 when . . ."

Aunty Toni keeps talking to Momma, but I'm lost in my thoughts. When we're backstage, Brandon's eyes are always moving back and forth like he's reading something, like he can see the lines in his head. But now? His eyes look out of focus, like he can't see anything. Maybe he's sad about Tre, maybe it's something else, but it worries me, seeing him like this. I feel like I'm in the shower and I've breathed in too much steam. The inside of my head is starting to feel hot and my thoughts are sprinting past each other when Momma shakes me by the shoulder.

"Kel, baby? Are you all right?"

"Huh?"

"Your Aunty Toni asked you a question and you staring off like you seen a ghost. You feeling okay?"

I shake my head a little to clear the fog and hitch a grin onto my face to calm Momma. "Sorry, Aunty, what was the question?"

Aunty and Momma exchange a sidelong glance that looks eerily similar to the telepathic convo look me and

Brandon get sometimes. Always weird to remember that's where we got it from. They don't look convinced by my answer, but Aunty Toni asks again.

"I said, what you know about Earth, Wind and Fire, nephew?"

"They're . . . all elements in Avatar?" I say slowly.

Aunty Toni sucks her teeth. Okay, wrong answer, my bad.

"You see, Willow, kids these days don't know a perfect song! A perfect song lift you up from wherever you're at to wherever you need to go. Stirs your marrow up, and wherever you were when you heard it first, it can always take you back there. It ain't always God, but it's always holy. When you come back up here on Wednesday for family dinner, I'll show you a couple things, you hear?"

"Sounds like a plan, Aunty," I say.

Me and Momma pick up our plates and wave off Aunty Toni's usual "Oh, I'll get those" as we scrub them clean at the sink in silence. We say our goodbyes and walk the three flights of stairs down to our apartment. It's routine again. I tell Momma I'm tired and head to my room to read. But I'm not taking in a word of it, the words swimming in front of me like confused birds. I'm thinking about Brandon and how ever since we left Pastor Sweat's office he barely said three sentences. I'm thinking about how I've never seen the hard lines of his face like that unless someone brings up his dad, Uncle Jimmy. I'm thinking how a couple floors above us, the cinnamon candle must be burning low, sputtering and flickering like always. But for the first time in our sad routine, Brandon looks afraid, like the shadows over him are growing and the light is running out.

Wednesday starts as a gray spill of morning. I wrestle an old orange Nike hoodie over my head and slip upstairs before Momma wakes up. It's been two whole days since I heard anything from Brandon besides "hit you back later" or just "in studio." Not that B isn't ever busy, but Brandon *always* hits me back within a couple of hours. I'm starting to get worried.

When I get to Brandon's room, I knock softly.

No answer.

I knock again. Still nothing.

The third knock finally gets a distant-sounding "Come in." When I do, I find the floor blanketed with crumpled up pages. I walk toward Brandon, sitting at his desk erasing something, paper crinkling around my shoes like badly drawn snowflakes.

"Oh, Kel. What's good, cuzzo?" Brandon smiles weakly.

"Man, what's good with *you*?" I shoot back, a little louder than I mean to.

"What you getting so buck for?" Brandon cocks an eyebrow.

"You been ghost for days, fam. Something's up, so can you stop frontin and tell me what the problem is?"

It's quiet in the room then, aside from the drumming of Brandon's pen against the desk as we stare at each other. My heart feels like it's trying to punch its way out my chest, and I have that too-much-steam feeling in my head again. Honestly, me and Brandon *never* beef. I don't even know if this is beef, I just know I've never had to beg him to let me in like this. Finally, his shoulders slump.

"I got nothing, fam. The song, I got nothing. Like, zero."

"Dang." I feel a wave of heat pass under my skin and my mouth go dry. "I mean, how many times have you tried?"

"This many." Brandon's voice is stiff as a board as he gestures around the floor. "But they all keep coming out just . . . flat. Like I don't want to write one of them verses where it's like '*Things are messed up, whole country falling apart, but also jazz exists so it's all good!*'

y'know? I just don't know, Kel. Words just . . . never been so hard to find, you feel me?"

"I do," I mumble, remembering that sawdust in the throat feeling I get when I can't get the right words for my own rhymes, and I don't even show those to anybody. I wish I knew how to help. I've never seen Brandon's eyes so bloodshot. If only . . .

Wait.

"What if I helped you?" I hear myself ask.

"With what?" Brandon cocks an eyebrow. "With the song?"

"Yeah, maybe I could write some bars for it, and you could build on it. You already got Prodigious working on the beat, right?" I feel pins and needles all over my body as I get more excited about the idea.

"I don't know, Kel." He sucks his teeth and drums the pencil harder. "Your pen is wild, but we only got a couple days."

"Which is all the more reason you got nothing to lose by letting me at least try. Plus, Pastor Sweat never said you had to do it by yourself, he just said he needed a song. You'd do it for me," I shoot back, crossing my arms and accidentally dipping a finger into my kinda sweaty left armpit.

Puberty is so wack.

"Aight, fine, you can help, dawg," Brandon mutters.

"I'mma stay on it, tho. We'll talk on this more at family dinner tonight."

I nod, we do our secret handshake, and I step out into Aunty Toni's living room, where the first creamy rays of a new day crack the gray open like trumpets where there used to be quiet.

Later that night, me and Brandon finish washing the dishes in silence and trudge back into the living room to sit next to our moms. I tried all day to write the song but it felt like there was static gumming up my brain every time I tried putting a pen to it. I didn't have to ask Brandon—it was all in his eyes the minute Aunty Toni opened the door. What were we gonna do? The song needed to be in by Saturday so Pastor Sweat could go over the rhymes.

But as soon as we step out into the living room, horns burst out of the scratchy speaker like we're the president or something. Momma and Aunty are in the middle of the room dancing like there's no tomorrow. I look at Momma, and for once she's not just Momma—she's something about to take flight. Both of them are laughing, shining, dipping, swerving—they're a whole ocean of cool! My mom is . . . dope?!

"I told you we'd teach you something 'bout Earth, Wind and Fire, boy!" Aunty Toni booms.

"This is 'September'! It's my favorite song!" Momma chimes in, spinning and two-stepping.

"And one of the world's few *perfect* songs!" Aunty spins Momma, her dress kicking up around her ankles like a blooming flower. "You boys write anything like this, you good for life."

Watching them, I feel a surge of joy like a perfect seventy-seven-degree day, like I got the best parts of June on a loop. Sometimes you forget how much you love someone until you see them laugh. Right now, Momma isn't swollen joints and tired smiles, and it has me smiling ear to ear. Even I almost want to dance but I jam my hands in my pockets before Aunty can grab them and start spinning, because I only have rhythm on the page, feel me? Besides, it's enough just to watch all of us become the song one way or another. Brandon's foot tapping like a high hat and Aunty Toni's laugh blaring like trumpets, I'm humming a song I've never heard before. I know somehow, whenever I hear it again, it'll be able to take me right back here.

And then I feel a sharp elbow to my ribs.

I'm 'boutta glare at Brandon, but he's got that wide grin on his face like when he's got a plan forming. It dawns on me too, a warm feeling like Aunty Toni's cinnamon candles, like the first light of a good day: we gotta write the track about *this,* this feeling right now! We duck back into his bedroom without another word, and Brandon tosses me a spare notebook. I start writing before my pen even hits the page. It feels breezy, like what I imagine birds feel when they skim the surface of a lake, so fast and free that nothing can pull you down, not even your reflection.

"Kel, this verse is absolute flames!!" Brandon crows, punching the air. "I mean, I knew your pen was mad strong but, fam, this is absolutely your best work."

"Yeah, it all just sorta came to me."

"This is *love,* Kel. I think it even fits with some of the verse that I got on mines." Brandon flips through the pages, eyes darting between each notepad. "I can't take credit for this on my own, fam. You gotta come onstage with me to do this for the church concert!!"

The room goes fuzzy, and I can hear my heartbeat in my ears, ginger ale in my skull. The idea of me onstage in front of all those people steals all my chill. I try harder and harder to get a grip, breathe normal, but it's like trying to catch a lightning bug with your hands full.

"Kel? Kel?" Brandon is shaking my shoulder softly. "Hey, hey, I'm sorry. I forgot how you feel about being onstage. I just was trying to say thank you, but that don't mean you gotta do what I wanna do, aight? No matter what, we a team now. You got your superpower, and I got mines."

I know he means it, and I start to feel better. He's right—we don't both have to be onstage to make an impact. My words are enough.

I imagine Brandon spitting the new verse for the Black joy track in front of everyone from the congregation, the way Mr. Duke's little constellation of moles will crinkle and Aunty Toni will gleam with pride from head to toe. Brandon stomping from end to end of the stage with his hand swimming in front of him to keep time while the crowd sways their arms from side to side like they caught the spirit.

Our people with palms the color of elm and oak and not an ounce of ash, waving back at Brandon; our people, a whole forest that loves him back.

I think about how my verse and Brandon's flow will make the people we love most dance and grin and sing along, just like Momma and Aunty Toni out in the living room right now.

It's not jazz music but it is a kind of jazz, I think, to help people improvise, transform into a place where there aren't mistakes, only a masterpiece changing directions, and that makes the joy bloom in my chest all over again.

Brandon daps me up and I love his warm, sure

palm in my smaller one. I've looked at him my whole life, and we've always been enough. Sure as the moon needs the sun and the sun needs the moon, sure as birds think their reflections are swimming below them and the ocean thinks it can finally fly, we that kind of tight. And it makes the whole world feel a little more beautiful and a lot less quiet. The way I know my words will help Brandon move a crowd until they all bloom into bright teeth and swirling limbs—I love that the most.

Nothing will stop us. We everywhere now.

OUR DILL

BY JUSTIN A. REYNOLDS

It all starts when I lose my head.

No, I don't mean I lose my temper like *Ugh, I'm so mad Netflix canceled my favorite show AGAIN*—which actually *did* happen by the way; thanks, Netflix. When I say I lost my head, I mean I literally can't find my head.

I know what you're thinking—*Jay, you probably just misplaced it. Your head will turn up.* Except it's not that simple. I'm on the clock here—any minute and the basketball team will race out onto the court for warmups and they're gonna announce me and I gotta race out there and do my mascot thing. And look, I get it, some people don't care about the mascot, and those that do basically just wanna see me clown—like when I "accidentally" trip into the stands and fall into their laps, or when I toss a bucket of water onto our opposing fans (don't worry, at the last sec, I swap out water for blue confetti). The point is, it's important I locate my furry head immediately.

I'm in the middle of tossing my second large dirty-towel cart when a familiar voice says my name, temporarily pausing my frantic locker room search for my missing noggin.

"Gross, what are you doing walking around without a head, Jay?" Mia asks.

"You didn't get my text?"

Mia laughs. "I did. That's why I'm here. You know, in the boys' locker room."

"So then why aren't you freaking out with me?" I ask her. I point to the last dirty-towel hamper. "C'mon, if we work together we should be able to tip that one over and—"

Mia looks me up and down, then rotates her gaze around the now-ransacked locker room.

"Wait, what's that?"

"What's what?"

"I think there's something on your . . ."

"There's *what* on my *what*?" Listen, I love Mia. I really do. She's my best friend. But right now, Mia has me doing that thing where I'm spinning round and round trying to see what in the world she's pointing at from six feet away—which is time I can't really afford to waste because, umm, hello, I'm supposed to be head-hunting.

Mia takes a few steps closer, and motions toward my back. "*That.* Stuck to your . . ." She pauses and gives me

240

a weird smile as she purses her lips to let the final word rip. *"Booty."*

And I'm sorry but I can't help it; I explode in hysterical laughter because . . . *booty*. Look, I know you're all super eye-rolling me like *Really, J, dang, how immature can you be*. But I have never, ever been able to resist breaking out into uncontrollable, full-body-shaking, everybody-within-a-two-mile-radius-turn-around-to-look-at-what-all-that-noise-is-about, stomach-aching laughter at that word. Naturally, Mia, being my aforementioned best friend since the first day of kindergarten, *knows* this better than almost anyone and she likes—no, LOVES—to take advantage of my weakness. But also, say "booty" out loud and tell me you don't think it's funny.

When I finally regain control of my mouth and brain, I stop spinning long enough for Mia to pull off the object stuck to my butt and, surprise, turns out it's a half-eaten protein bar.

"So, do I even want to know how you've got a protein bar attached to your furry boo . . . bottom?" Mia asks, catching herself in time to spare me the bellyache.

I shrug. "Focus, please. What am I gonna do without my head, Mia?"

But before she can answer, before she can even part her lips, clear on the other side of the room we hear the loud grating screech of the boys' locker room door swing open, followed by an even louder, super confident, mysterious voice calling out:

"Hey, is there anyone in here missing a head by chance?"

Yep, that's when this whole thing officially began.

And by *whole thing officially began,* I mean when everything officially started turning to crap.

The owner of our ultra-cool mystery voice?

"Hi, I don't believe we've met," he says, smiling as if he literally *just* invented smiling right in this very moment. And already I don't like this dude's energy. I mean, who—under the age of seventy-eight—even talks like that? No, wait, that's an insult to old people—I know for a fact that my nana would not say that. Yet here this kid is—he can't be much older than Mia and I, if he's older at all—acting like he just stepped off the set of some 1920s black-and-white screwball comedy and into our lives.

"No, wait," he goes on, "I definitely know we haven't met. There's no way I could ever forget a face like yours." Yes, he actually said *those* words in *that* order. But the thing is, no matter how much I hate to admit it—and trust me I really, really hate to—somehow the kid pulls it off. It takes me all of three seconds to realize this guy has everything going for him.

First Thing Going for Him: his smooth, dark brown skin. Once upon a time, my skin was smooth—some might even say *cocoa-buttery*—but lately it's Acneville, population: me. It makes no sense, but my right cheek keeps breaking out into a pattern of three pimples in the same upside-down triangular formation as the finger holes in a bowling ball.

Second Thing Going for Him and probably the most important thing: overflowing confidence. I mean, the kid just said *I could never forget a face like yours* and it sounded *not* stupid! Yep, he definitely knows he's cool, exuding that easy confidence that I imagine all ridiculously attractive people are born with. Me, I don't know how to judge my looks except to say I'm probably the classic definition of EXTRAORDINARY. Wait, oops, that didn't come out right. I meant I'm the definition of EXTRA ORDINARY. See that space between those two words? All the difference.

"My name's Banks," he says, taking Mia's hand in his own.

Banks? His name is Banks? What kind of name is

that? Okay, well, that partially explains his vibe. With a name like Banks, of course he's into himself. Of course he's—

"Will Banks," he adds, *still* holding Mia's hand. For a hot second, I half-expect him to bring her hand to his lips for a black-hand-side smooch. Not that Mia would let him do that; Mia, the same girl who told off Jason Miller, the most popular kid in school and an *eighth grader* after he tried slipping his arm around her shoulders and asking for her *math*. At the time, I was confused why Jason wanted Mia's prealgebra homework—as far as I knew he was in eighth grade algebra—but apparently, Mia knew exactly what he meant because she replied: *I'm not giving you my number, Jason. And do not touch me without my permission, thanks.*

What do you mean I can't have your number? You serious? And then, looking at me, he'd cracked a big grin and a look of disbelief. *Please don't tell me this dude's your boyfriend.*

And I was thrown off—not just because, to my knowledge, no one had ever accused Mia and me of being together as anything more than best friends—but also because rather than fire back a quick reply as she'd done only seconds earlier, Mia hesitated and looked at me. But why? What did she want me to say? She knew as well as I did that we weren't boyfriend and girlfriend—not even close. I mean, there'd been that one time in second grade when we'd been each other's school valentines but that was about it. And yes, we told each other everything; there were no secrets between us. If one of us was in trouble, we came to the other. When we had good news to share, we couldn't wait to tell each other before we told anyone else. And yeah, when she starred in the school production of *My Fair Lady,* of course I'd sat front-row center for every weekend show that month. And yes, she rode all the roller coasters with me at Cedar Point every summer, even the whirly ones that sometimes made her dizzy. But even still, I couldn't tell *what* she wanted me to say—did she want me to say something at all?

Of course she did, you silly boy, my sister, Jules, told me later when I recounted the story to her.

But what was I supposed to say? I protested.

Whatever was on your heart, Jules said. Which I admit is kinda genius, but also easier said than done. Ugh.

"I'm Mia Landry," Mia says, seemingly not very bothered by the fact that this Will Banks guy was *still* clutching her hand. What was going on—did he have superglue on his palm and fingers? Did they need me to unstick them? Should I offer?

I wait for Mia to introduce me—because that's what we always do, intro each other. But that doesn't seem to be on her mind.

"Hey," I say, with a small wave. "I'm J—"

But Will interrupts me. "Mia, that's beautiful."

Okay, too far. This guy has no idea who he's talking to—he's definitely crossed the line of no return. No way Mia is gonna let this slide when she—

"Thank you," she says, her cheeks suddenly rosy. Since when did her cheeks get rosy? I've known her for seven years and this is the first time I've seen this happen—maybe it's just a coincidence. Maybe Mia's cheeks glowing is a once-every-seven-year phenomenon like some comet falling or a planet suddenly appearing brightly in the sky. "I've never met a Will before."

"It's actually William . . . ," he begins.

Maybe I should jump in. Maybe that's what Mia's waiting for. Maybe she already signaled me to intervene but I missed it in all of my missing mascot head anxiety. Maybe I should interject right now with *Sorry, Will, William, whatever you call yourself, but Mia's not interested . . .*

"Five, five, five, eight, three," Mia's saying. Wait, those numbers—so familiar. Did she just—that's her phone number. But why is she saying it out loud? And why is he typing into his phone? Obviously I've missed something. Something super important.

"Seven, five," I blurt.

And Will gives me a look but I watch his fingers tap the 7 and 5 on his screen.

"Uhh, that's *not* my number," Mia says. "Seven, six. You don't know my number by heart?"

"Oh, you know how I always mix up my fives and sixes."

Mia gives me a look that says, *No, you don't.*

"Anyway," she says, turning back to Will. "Just text me."

"Wait, what are we texting about?" I ask.

Neither Will nor Mia answers me, so I grab Will's phone. "Here, let me just put my number in, too, so we can group text."

"Oh," Will says. "Uh, cool, bro."

Wait, did Mia just roll her eyes? Was that eye roll aimed at me? Or was it aimed at me but about Will, like *Can you believe this guy is making me give him my number, gross.*

"I heard there was a dance in a couple of weeks," Will says. "You going?"

"Of course we're going," I jump in, knowing he's not asking me.

Mia nods. "Probably."

"Cool," Will says.

"Cool," Mia says.

The three of us just stand there a moment, saying nothing.

And then I hear the one sound that means my time is up:

The roar of the crowd as the announcer calls out the basketball team one by one. In less than ninety seconds I'm supposed to be cartwheeling across that hardwood. Technically, I should've already been out there fifteen minutes ago for warm-ups. The crowd loved my warm-up routine. I was responsible for getting everyone hype. Without me, who was going to send the entire student body into a wild frenzy? Who was gonna come tearing through the paper banner held tight by the cheerleaders on either side, before sliding to my knees in a dramatic flourish, before playing a killer chord on air guitar? That always made Mia laugh, my air guitar. Honestly, that's one of the main reasons why I do it.

"My head," I say, breaking the silence.

"Huh?" Will says.

I motion toward the big furry head in his hands. "I'm gonna need my head. I got a show to put on. They won't start without me."

"Oh, right," Will says, handing it over. His face scrunches. "I don't mean to be rude, but what are you supposed to be?"

And this makes me laugh—because duh, clearly this

guy isn't the sharpest pencil in the pencil box. "I'm a pickle."

"Oh, well, that's quite a pickle, isn't it," Will says, grinning, except he's looking at Mia.

"Dill with it," Mia retorts.

And they're cracking up and I'm trying to think of another pickle joke, but it's harder than you might think. The announcer's voice crackles over the locker room speaker. "And now, everyone's favorite mascot . . ."

"That's me," I say, nodding. I throw Will my best smile—the one that says *I'm onto you* but also *I'm not at all worried, bud.* "I'm kind of a big dill."

"What?" both Mia and Will say simultaneously.

Okay, maybe I'm a *little* worried.

Mia looks up at me with a pink nose and I laugh, tap my nose. It's a Mia-Jay tradition—after every game we slide into a booth at Kate's Diner for fries and milkshakes—chocolate for her, strawberry for me.

"There's shake all over my face, isn't there?" she asks.

I shrug. "Not *all* over."

I wet a napkin in my untouched glass of water and pass it to her. I watch her as she wipes her face. "You can't take me anywhere," she says, laughing at herself.

"I'd take you anywhere," I hear myself say.

She looks up at me, her formerly pink nose pinched together. "What did you say?"

Did I really just say that out loud? I shake my head with the same velocity as a dog after an unwanted bath. "Nothing. Just talking to myself."

She studies me, then nods and goes back to staring at her lap. More specifically at the thing in her lap, which she now holds up for me to see. "Why hasn't he texted me yet?"

So that's why she's being so weird. Why on the drive here with Jules and two of her friends—me and Mia in the backseat as usual with me voluntarily taking the middle seat because it makes Mia carsick—she'd kept waking up her phone screen and then sighing as if it was somehow disappointing her. She wanted him to text her. She was thinking about him. Somehow even when he wasn't here, he was still *here*—which is maybe worse than him physically being here.

And I don't know why I answer her like this—I mean, if I thought about it, I could probably tell you why, but I don't want to think about it because honestly I'm not proud of what I tell her—

"Guy like that, he probably gets numbers from girls all the time." And as if that wasn't bad enough, I double down on my rudeness with: "It probably wasn't that big of a deal to him, meeting us." And yeah, even though I say *us,* we both know I mean *you.*

And I expect her to fire back at me, to put me in my place, but instead her face droops a little and she says nothing, and I feel awful because the last thing I want is for her to be hurt . . . not by this Will guy, but definitely not by me. My mouth's open to apologize when her phone buzzes. She taps the notification excitedly, and then her face lights up.

"He texted me," she says. "It's him!"

I force a smile. "Oh, cool," I say, trying to make my voice as casual as possible. "What did he say?"

She grins and holds out her phone screen to me.

WILL: Hey

"What should I say back?"

"Hey?"

"Ohmigod, Mia, duh." She nods enthusiastically. "You're so smart, Jay. Thanks."

And I want to say *obviously not as smart as you think* but instead I just watch her fingers find the letters . . . *H . . . e . . . y.* She pauses, glances up, chewing on her lip the way she does when she's really thinking hard about something. I see the lightbulb pop on above her head as she giggles and taps another word to go with her *Hey—*

You.

"Sooo, you think it's weird if I ask him to the dance?" she asks me four days later, plopping her tray onto the cafeteria table next to my bag lunch.

I consider asking *who* but I'm over that game now. Besides, for the past ninety-six hours, it's like Will's the only subject she's interested in.

Not only that, she wanted to ask him to the dance.

Not just that, it's our first real dance.

And although we hadn't exactly discussed it, I assumed we'd go together. The way we always did things.

"I don't know," I answer her. I realize I'm saying that a lot these few days—*I don't know.*

Do you think Will likes hot or cold cereal?

I don't know.

Do you think Will was really cool at his last school, too?

I don't know.

And then the weirdest, most unexpected thing happens—my normally confident best friend doubts herself. "He probably already has a date. I mean, even if he doesn't why would he wanna go with me when he could go with anyone he wanted? I heard Sarah Mitchell and Jasmine Sawyer talking about how cute the new guy is."

"Oh," I say, because I'm unsure what else to say. Because suddenly it's like I'm talking to an alien who I've only just met.

"Oh?" she parrots. "Did you hear what I said, Jay? *Sarah Mitchell* and *Jasmine Sawyer*. They're the hottest two girls in seventh grade."

"They're okay, I guess."

"Okay you guess?" She shakes her head in disbelief. "Shut up. You said you'd walk on hot coals for Jasmine."

A simple game we play. Hot Coals. Basically, someone says something like *Wow, Jasmine Sawyer is super cute*. And then the other person says, *Okay, but hot coals?* Meaning, would you walk over a bed of hot coals to get with her? Weird, I know. Obviously, it's an exaggeration—a way to ask *How much are you willing to do for this person or thing?* The game started after we watched a documentary in social studies about rituals. Apparently, hot-coal walking is all the rage in a few places around the world.

"Maybe I take it back," I say.

But Mia doesn't believe me. "Why would you take it back? You've had like a secret crush on her since third grade."

I nod. "Things change."

"What things?" she asks.

"Feelings," I say, surprising myself. And the word just hangs between us, both of us embarrassed by my response but also neither of us sure why or what to do about it.

Which is why I open my big mouth and say the dumbest thing I think I've ever said.

"Wait, let me get this straight," Jules says when I explain the situation. "You told Mia, the girl that you like, that you'd help her get with this Will guy?"

I shake my head, hold up my hands like *whoa, whoa.* "First of all, Mia and I are best friends, that's it. Secondly, I'm helping her the same way she'd help me. You know, because we're . . ."

"Best friends, got it," Jules says, laughing. "Well, good luck with that plan, lil bro. But I still think it might be easier if you just told Mia . . ."

Her voice trails off.

At the worst possible time. Because I had the sense that whatever came next was the singular most important piece of advice anyone would ever give me. And I didn't just want it. I was desperate for it. I needed it. I *need* it.

Except my sister doesn't seem to have the same urgency. "It might be easier if I told Mia what?"

"Never mind," Jules says, already headed upstairs for her room. "It's none of my business."

"But it is," I call up to her. "I'm making it your business. Consider it your business." But it's too late, her bedroom door already closing behind her.

Which, typical. Siblings always wanna be in your business when you don't want them to be—so quick to give you their opinion on everything when it's the last thing you want—but then when you finally invite them in, when you ask them for their take, they're all *No, no, I'd hate to butt in.*

Like, make up your mind, you know? Is consistency too much to ask for?

I'm in fourth period study hall when the opportunity I've been dreading presents itself.

Mia's in art during this period, meaning I usually get a library pass and bury myself in a book recommendation from Ms. Bennett or Mr. Evecheck, the two coolest librarians ever. It's the only time Mia and I aren't together, mainly because I'm about as artistic as a brick.

But the library is closed for an eighth-grade presentation, so I have to sit in regular study hall. That's when I hear—

"Yeah, so, I don't know how to choose, you know?" says a voice from outside that I recognize. I crane my neck from my chair to see if it really is who I think it is. "I mean, Jasmine and Sarah are both pretty hot. How do I even decide?" Yep, it's him all right—Will Banks in gym shorts and a white T-shirt, standing in the grass talking to our gym teacher, Mr. Kowalski, while the rest of his gym class kick a soccer ball up and down the pitch. Why Will was getting advice from our prehistoric gym teacher, I don't even know.

"I feel like this is something you should ask someone your own age," our gym teacher says. "But I wouldn't decide based on who's hotter."

Will shrugs. "It's not *just* that."

But Mr. Kowalski is lifting his whistle to his lips. "Okay, change sides," he calls out.

I raise my hand for a bathroom pass. It's not hard sneaking out the back door and around to the other side of the school—which is kind of worrisome how easy it is, but that's a different topic for a different day.

"Hey, Will," I say, motioning for him to come over to the sideline where I wait. He waves and then jogs over.

"Sup, bro," he says, smiling.

"Mia," I blurt.

His eyebrows raise. "What?"

"Forget Jasmine Sawyer and Sarah Mitchell, okay? You should take Mia. Mia Landry. She's your best option."

He frowns and for a moment I feel the pang of failure. He scratches his head, rubs his chin. "But don't you have a thing for Mia?"

Out of all the possible replies he could've given, this one I am least prepared for. "Huh? What? Me? And Mia? Ha-ha. No way. Ha-ha. Nope. We're just ... ha ... friends."

He tilts his chin like he's debating whether or not he believes me. Or maybe he's just wondering why I'm suddenly stuttering and drooling all over myself.

He shrugs. "Well, I do think Mia's cool. You think she'd go with me?"

My head nods. It feels like I've floated out of my body and I'm watching myself make weird choices that are definitely not in my own best interests. I could easily squash any shot of Mia and Will going to the dance together right now. Easily. *Nope, no chance, I was joking. She hates you. Definitely take Sarah.*

"Just ask her, Will," I say. "Just ask."

And I don't know why I helped Will. I guess it's less about helping him and more about helping Mia. And those feelings, those reasons, are way easier to figure out.

Mom and Dad make a big production about it, even though they both promised not to—

"Humor us," Mom says. "It's your first dance."

"Maybe my last dance, if I have to do a photo shoot every time," I grumble as Dad snaps yet another *candid shot;* this time of me rubbing that area just below my nose so that it probably looks like I've only just finished picking it. Ugh. I can see the Instagram caption now: *Our son digging in his nose for the last time before his first dance #TheTimeFliesBy #OurBabyIsn'tABaby #He'llAlwaysBeOurBabyBeQuietAndMindYourOwn BusinessThanks #We'reNotCryingYou'reCrying.*

"Oh hush, son," Dad says. He only calls me son when he gives me one-word instructions, like *hush,* or *sit,* or *lawnmower.*

Jules fixes my tie. Licks her finger, then tries to put that same gross wet finger onto my face. Naturally, I jerk away from her.

"You have something in the corner of your eye," Jules says.

I rub my own eye. "Next time just say that," I say, extracting a piece of fuzz. "Also, I don't see why you thought saliva was necessary for fuzz removal."

Thirty minutes later, the three of them wave excitedly at me from the car as I walk to the door and press the doorbell. My heart is pounding in my chest in ways it's never pounded. Pounding so hard I nearly turn back and yell across the yard, over at the driveway where Mom's minivan awaits to escort us to the dance, *Hey, can seventh graders have heart attacks?* But then the door flies open.

"You look great, Jay," she says.

My mouth is suddenly dry and cottony but somehow I manage to choke out the words "Thanks. You do, too, Jasmine."

Jasmine puts on a ginormous pair of neon green sunglasses and I plop a big purple wig onto my head and the photographer keeps saying, "Lean in closer, guys, closer," until our cheeks are basically touching—we're standing in front of a fake tropical island backdrop with a giant orange fake sun in the top corner, which is appropriate because I wonder if Jasmine feels the heat radiating from my face, if she can see the steam wafting from it the way you sometimes see clouds of smoke float up from the sewer grilles in the street.

As I'm handing the photographer the twenty-dollar bill Mom slipped me, I notice Will in line and for a moment I'm afraid and angry and sad, all at once. *How could he come without her? How could he take a picture without her? How could he even—*

But then I hear a familiar laugh and Will takes a few steps to his right and now I see everything—I see Mia, standing there, grinning in her brilliant blue dress, a pale yellow flower pinned near her right shoulder. I'm debating if I should go over and say hello when Jasmine hands me our photo. We're smiling. We look happy.

"You thirsty?" I ask her.

We grab punch and it takes all of my concentration to not pour it all over us as I lift the ladle from the bowl and tilt it toward our clear plastic cups. My hand is shaking because of course my body is turning against me, wants to see me embarrass myself, and I wait for Jasmine to laugh but she just steadies my hand with hers and beams at me.

"Are you nervous?" she asks me. But she doesn't say it like an accusation. More like a secret we're sharing.

Still, I consider lying because I don't want her to think I'm a loser, because I don't want her to think I don't know how to be at a dance with someone I think is pretty cool, but instead I nod. "A little."

"Me too. A little," she says. "Good thing we already got our first hug out the way."

I scrunch my face, confused. We've already hugged? How had I missed this? She pulls up a picture on her phone. It's at one of our games; it's me, dressed as mascot Dillon Pickle sandwiched—pun intended—between a dozen students. And who's cheesing beside me with her arm wrapped around my fuzzy green shoulders? Yep, Jasmine.

"So, see," Jasmine says. "We've already got the scary stuff outta the way."

And then she takes my hand and leads me through a sea of kids onto the dance floor, just in time for the latest dance craze everyone's doing online. Naturally, I don't know how to do it. My shoulders are too stiff. My rhythm too nonexistent.

"Watch," Jasmine says. "It seems hard but it's really just three steps."

And I watch her and I try to follow but somehow I keep turning it into seventeen steps. Even still, I can't lie—I'm having fun.

So, of course, a slow song comes on next. "This is easier," Jasmine says, winking. "It's just two steps."

And I'm not great at it but also, I'm not the worst. And I realize how good Jasmine smells. And how her eyes get so big when she's excited and how her nose wiggles when we're teasing each other. "I'm glad you asked me," she says.

"Me too," I say.

Out of the corner of my eye, I catch a glimpse of my best friend, dancing with her date, her back to me as they move in a slow steady circle. And for a moment, I think we're gonna miss each other again, that by the time Mia's facing my way I'll be turned the other way, Jasmine aimed at her instead.

But then I realize, no, we're gonna catch each other just right and I can't explain it but my stomach flip-flops and I panic—because maybe I don't wanna meet eyes like this. I start to turn away, but Mia's eyes catch mine, and she waves at me. I grin hard at her and she grins right back. And because I'm corny I shoot her the thumbs-up sign, which she smartly does not return. She does me one better: her mouth opens but no sound comes out. Still, I know exactly what she's saying. *I'd walk over hot coals for you.*

Save me a dance, I mouth back.

And she does, and it feels good, dancing with someone who is just as bad at dancing as I am. And also, it just feels good.

PERCIVAL AND THE JAB

BY P. DJÈLÍ CLARK

There's a Jab living in my closet. I don't mean some man in shorts and wearing a Viking helmet like at Carnival. That would be creepy. No, I mean a *real* Jab—glistening black with curving white horns on his head. I first noticed him on the plane, when my mother came to take me back to America. Just like that, I got a new set of grown-ups and a baby sister to boot. But one story at a time. Anyway, I look up and there he is, contorted between some luggage and grinning down at me. He follows us through customs and I glimpse white trousers and a barbed tail as he dives into the trunk of our car. When we get home, he moves into my closet. And he's been there ever since.

"Lewee goh outside nah? Tired coop up here like fowl!"

Did I mention the Jab complains? C-o-n-s-t-a-n-t-l-y. He follows me everywhere, getting into mischief. Once at a restaurant in Brooklyn he stuck his whole face into a pot of oil down. Another time on the train he started jooking people with his pitchfork, laughing when they jumped. At a store he turned the speakers up all the way to blast a soca tune. And I get blamed each time.

"I'm fine right here," I say, watching television. Back in Trinidad I mostly had BBC. In America, there are more channels than I can count.

"We goh pitch marble wit neighbor son!" He hops atop the TV, rattling the chains crisscrossing his bare chest to get my attention. "Or look for crapaud in dee canal!" His mouth stretches into a sharp smile, eyes bright.

"This isn't Chaguanas. And I'm ten now. Too old to play marbles or in that dirty canal."

The Jab's smile drops. "We should goh back home."

"This is my home now," I retort. "Why don't you go back?"

He doesn't answer.

◦ ◦ ◦

"Cereal again?" The Jab fumes at my breakfast. "What happen to saltfish? Zabuca? Bake?" He scrunches up his face. "And why lately yuh talking funny so?"

"I'm not talking funny. This is how people talk in America."

He does a handstand on the counter. "Schupedness. Yuh sound like ah Yankee."

"Good. I'm supposed to."

His mouth makes a long "steuuuuuuups." He doesn't like my attempts at being American. But what does he know? School here starts in a few weeks. They're talking about putting me back a grade. My mother isn't having any of it. She makes me watch the news each day to talk like they do; Americans think people with accents aren't as smart, she explains.

We meet with the principal—a man in a suit with slick hair that looks wet. My mother's all smiles as they talk, flicking on her American like a light switch. The Jab is here of course, pretending to gag.

"Percival." The principal smiles at me. "So you're to be our newest pupil?"

"Yes," I answer in my best American.

"You learned English back in your native country?"

I frown and nod. What does he think people speak in Trinidad?

"Can you recite the alphabet?"

I almost laugh as I do. What ten-year-old can't recite the alphabet?

"And his reading skills? We expect higher than what is common in the third world."

My mother's face tightens, but her smile holds. She looks to a shelf.

"Oh no, those are my professional texts. My secretary can get—"

But my mother's already selected a thick book. Setting it down, she opens and points. I walk over, looking at the page. The Jab, hanging upside down by his tail from the light fixture, sneers. As I read, the principal's eyebrows rise. I don't understand it all, but sounding out the words is easy. Would go better if the Jab stopped shaking his chains and singing:

Tingalayo! Come, little donkey, come!
Tingalayo! Come, little donkey, come!
Me donkey walk, me donkey talk,
Me donkey eat wit knife and fork!

"Nice Jab."

I look up in surprise. With just weeks before school, I'm walking about the apartments my family lives in—hoping to find some other kids. I don't expect the one person to wave at me to be a woman almost my mother's age, standing by a doorway in a long red dress. I certainly don't expect her to see the Jab trailing me like a shadow.

"I said nice Jab," she repeats when I come over, her singsong accent tickling my ears. "And yes, I can see him fine. My name Miss Marabella. I sell sweeties." She nods to her open door and I hesitate. My parents warned that strangers could be dangerous here. Only, she can see the Jab. And that's big. I step inside and a thud follows from behind me. I turn to see the Jab pressed against an invisible wall. He tries again but hits it once more.

"No Jab in me house," Miss Marabella says, closing the door in his face. I smile. No one's ever done that! The brown skin around her cheeks lifts as she leans down to smile at me, and I catch familiar scents from back home—mauby root, wet earth after a heavy rain, and soursop. "You want some sweeties?" I nod. Who doesn't? She seats me at a small table before disappearing. A scuffling sound makes me look up, where a small girl is peeking from the stairs.

"My daughter," Miss Marabella says, returning. "She shy." She sets down a plate heaped with sweeties—sugary tamarind balls, guava cheese, coconut fudge. My stomach growls and I begin stuffing my mouth.

She laughs. "You talk like ah Yankee, but yuh belly full Trini."

"Have you always been able to see?" I ask between chews. "Like I do?"

Miss Marabella nods. "Make two of we with that gift, ent?"

I nod back. My grandmother was the one who

explained my "gift." She can see too. Back home, she taught me how to look for the things others couldn't— witches out at night who make dogs start barking, soucouyant streaking in a fireball, looking to suck your breath away, little douen people with backward feet, and more. She also taught me rules—about not sleeping the same direction of the dead, unless you want jumbie in your bed. To stay away from cemeteries at night, where Lajabless the cowfoot woman and monstrous Lagahoo lurk. And to *never* say the name of the Chief Devil (Bazil, whose palace is in a giant silk-cotton tree) three times and truly mean it, lest you call him up!

"What's your name?" Miss Marabella asks.

"Percival," I answer.

"Percival," she repeats. "The Trini boy with a Yankee accent. How that happen?"

"I got sent to live with my grandparents when I was small."

"Ohh. One of those, eh? Now your mother and father bring you back."

I nod. "Where in Trinidad are you from?"

She grins. "Arima. I come here to find new work. Didn't like my boss. So I fool him and leave, without telling."

I look out the window to the Jab, who's drooling at the sweeties. "Why is he here?"

"That for you to find out," Miss Marabella replies. "But be mindful. Jab dem can be mischievous, dangerous creatures. Watch you don't lose control of him."

Outside, the Jab puts on a devilish grin, his sharp teeth gleaming.

It's my sister's birthday. She's three. The Jab sniffs the air, sensing the fete to come. He begs and whines to attend but I say no. I promise to bring him food—only if he behaves.

That afternoon, family arrives from all over. I endure hugs and Polaroids. From time to time I sneak upstairs, keeping my promise. The Jab is a bottomless pit. Roti, cookup, stew chicken, currants roll, and more go down his gullet. And he's still hungry!

"You want what?" It's my tenth trip.

"Just ah drink, little little," he pleads, rubbing his thumb and forefinger together.

"They won't let me have a drink."

"Then sneak it nah. Do so, and I leave you be."

I sigh. It's late. I'm tired. And the birthday party is now a full fete, for adults only.

"Fine. But that's it!"

I sneak downstairs and back up with a bottle of rum

that's near empty. The Jab grins. He pours a bit into the cap, offering it.

"Come nah, take ah little drink."

"I can't."

"Why?"

"I'm ten?"

"But it sweet, sweet," he purrs. "Take ah taste."

I bite my lip. Taking the cap, I sniff and make a face. People drink this? I push it back.

"No thanks."

The Jab shrugs. He tilts the bottle back and gulps— shivering to make his chains rattle. I roll my eyes, then lie down to sleep.

It's much later when I wake up. I can hear people— laughing, shouting. My eyes go to the clock. Past three a.m. How long is this party going? A sudden sound makes me sit straight up. A conch shell. And my closet door is wide open. Empty.

Jumping from bed I make it out my room and half-way downstairs before I stop.

The world's gone crazy.

People are dancing, wildly, jumping and winding up their hips. Their clothes are smeared in syrup and birth-day cake and soil from potted plants. Someone's beating spoons on bottles and pots. I see my parents, their eyes glazed over like the rest. An uncle is the one blowing the conch shell, calling out while people shout in answer.

Oy yo yoi!

Aye ya yi!

Oy yo yoi!

Aye ya yi!

Then I see the Jab.

He's the eye of this storm, his body and arms swaying in a dance. All the people move with him, like he's the conductor of a mad orchestra. I rush down, pushing my way through.

"Stop it!"

The Jab ignores me.

I reach to yank his arm and he shoves me back. "Leave me lone nah!"

He laughs as the music grows louder, his dark lips spitting flames into the air.

For the first time, he is truly terrifying.

I reach for him again—grabbing at his chains. He howls, but stumbles along as I drag him back upstairs. When we reach the top I look down.

The conch blowing and chanting has stopped. People stare around in confusion, coming out of their daze. My mother wails when she sees the wreckage of our house. I pull the Jab into my room, shutting the door.

"What was that?" I ask angrily.

The Jab kisses his teeth. "Allyuh forget how to fete or whut? Allyuh come here and lose everyting! Lose who allyuh is!"

"I know who I am!" I shoot back. "I don't want to hear any more about back home! Just go away! All you do is cause me trouble! Go away!"

The Jab is quiet. Turning, he walks into the closet and slams the door behind him.

"You must get rid of that Jab," Miss Marabella says.

I'm sitting at her table, glumly crunching some kurma. It's the Monday after the party. My parents don't suspect me of anything. But they found the empty rum bottle in my room. And that didn't go well.

"I don't know what to do." I look to the Jab, who paces outside the window. "School starts soon, and if he follows me there . . ." I shudder, thinking of all the trouble the Jab will get into. What he'll get *me* into.

"Maybe I can help." She gets up and goes to the back. My eyes flick to the stairs, where I glimpse her daughter—who promptly runs away. Strange girl. When Miss Marabella returns, she's holding something small and black.

I stare at the molasses treat. "A toolum?" I ask.

"This toolum special. Give it to yuh Jab." I reach out but she pulls back. "You do this, you does have to *mean* it, hear? It not going to work otherwise."

I nod, taking the toolum. I plan on meaning it very much.

That night, I knock on my closet door. The Jab pokes his head out.

"Got you something." I hold out the toolum. "You always wanting sweeties. Here."

The Jab's eyes go big. He snatches the toolum, stuffing it in his mouth. I breathe in relief.

The next day the Jab isn't gone. But there's something strange to him. He's still sucking on that toolum for one, working hard too. He's so consumed by it, he doesn't bother to follow me. He just sits in the closet, sucking away. Another day goes by and I notice he's thinner, his skin and eyes gone dull. Three more days and I can see his ribs. He's almost sagging under his chains and his trousers fit him baggy. I'm surprised I'm not happier. I want to see him go, but watching him waste away like this is troubling. Like I'm losing something. A week after giving him the cursed toolum, I lie in bed at night staring at my closet, listening to that constant sucking—wondering if anything will be left of the Jab come morning.

"Percy . . . Perrrrciivaaal."

I wake up, thinking it's the Jab. But this is a woman's voice—someone standing over me.

"Miss Marabella?" I ask in surprise.

She smiles, and I'm wondering if this is a dream—but then I catch those familiar scents of home and I know I'm awake. But why is she here? How did she get into my room?

"Percival, I wanted to come and thank you."

Thank me? A small face peeks out from behind her red dress—her daughter.

Miss Marabella hums. "I come here all the way from Arima, so I can do my business how I want. This place have so much sweetness for me. Then you show up with that Jab. And I know he gon' be trouble. Take a while, but I figure out a way to be rid of him—thanks to you."

Now I'm more confused. "Why would the Jab be trouble for you?"

She smiles in a way that's no longer pleasant. "Because me and devils don't get along. And he not the only wicked thing come up here from Trinidad." Then, just like that, she steps out of her skin. It's like she was wearing a suit that fell off along with her clothes. What's standing before me now is shaped like a woman, but made up all of fire.

"You know what I am?" the fire woman asks.

I nod, my eyes wide. A soucouyant! A fire vampire who steals the breath from children! This whole time, Miss Marabella was a spirit too!

The soucouyant cackles. "Allyuh children is so sweet. Sweeter than my sweeties. And you, little Trini boy who want to be American so bad—you have a special sweetness I can't wait to taste. When I finish, I gon' find your little sister and eat she up too. Don't bother screaming. I make it so everybody sleep. It's just you and me."

I'm shaking. But I manage to talk. "You got that wrong. It's not just you and me."

The soucouyant frowns before the Jab lashes her with his chains. She was so busy gloating, she didn't see him limp from the closet. She shrieks when those chains hit her and spins about. The Jab is standing there, frail but not gone. I jump up on my bed, never knowing I could be so happy to see him again. Then I remember the toolum.

"Spit it out!" I yell. He tries but can't. The soucouyant screeches and her daughter flies at the Jab. Not a girl I realize now, a douen! It jumps up with backward feet to land on the Jab, biting and scratching black flakes from his skin.

"Spit out the toolum!" I cry again. But he can't—and

it's keeping him weak. No, keeping *us* weak. Why I've been feeling so troubled lately. Because he's not just a Jab. He's *my* Jab.

Thinking hard, I imagine chewing the toolum and can suddenly taste it in my mouth—sweet sugar and dark molasses with bits of coconut coating my tongue. Its cursed magic tries to take hold of me. Suddenly all I want to do is to try to get at the heart of it, sucking forever and ever. But no! I won't let it! Instead I force myself to stop and imagine spitting it out.

The toolum flies from my Jab's mouth and we both whoop!

In moments his skin is shiny and black again, dripping and boiling with syrupy goo, as he grows before my eyes. A clawed hand flings away the douen. Then he rounds on the soucouyant, holding a pitchfork as his barbed tail twitches. She screeches and roars into flames—as the two clash!

Their fight rages across my bedroom—my Jab with his pitchfork and the soucouyant hurling fireballs. The walls rattle and I wonder if they might not bring the whole apartment down. My Jab is a wonder to watch, but he's still weak. And it's not just from the toolum, I realize. It's me, trying so hard to forget who I was to be someone new here. I've made him weaker too. The soucouyant cackles.

"No devil can hold me! I leave that fool me boss and work for me own self!"

I blink. Her boss. That can only be one person. And I know how to call him.

Closing my eyes, I do what my grandmother warned I should never do—saying his name three times and truly meaning it. "Bazil! Bazil! Bazil!"

A whoosh of green flames flares, and the Chief Devil of the Silk-Cotton Tree appears in my bedroom. He's as fearsome as I imagined, a tall and broad monster in a red suit. He pushes up a red bowler sitting between two horns and plucks a thick cigar from his jaws. "Who fool enough to call up Bazil, Chief Devil of—" He stops, noticing my Jab and the soucouyant—who have both gone still. "What happening here?"

"Mr. Bazil!" I blurt out. "I called you up. To do you a favor."

Bazil's fiery eyes look me up and down. "You? Do ah favor for me? What nonsense yuh talking?"

"I hear you the Chief Devil," I reply. "That you the boss over every Jab, witch, and spirit." My chin jerks to the soucouyant. "You know what she tell me? That she come here from Arima. That she left without permission and fooled her old boss. You that fool, Mr. Bazil?"

The Chief Devil's eyes narrow at the soucouyant, who shrinks back.

"Allyuh think I does make joke?" He snaps his fingers. "Bookman!"

A second devil appears in another burst of green flames. The Bookman! His pink skin stands out, even among his fancy silk robes of every color imaginable, with two small batwings flapping on his back. His head is enormous. Too big for even his tall body, with a pointy black beard, pointy ears, and two small pointy horns.

"Bookman, is there a missing soucouyant from Arima making a fool of me?" Bazil asks.

The Bookman opens a giant leather-bound book, its pages flipping in a blur before they stop. He reads for a bit; then his blue eyes shift to the soucouyant. "You are not where you are supposed to be."

Bazil's eyes now grow bright with rage. Instead of roaring he inhales. The soucouyant shrieks, trying to flee. But she flies toward Bazil's open mouth, and he swallows her up! The Chief Devil belches, and I think I hear her still screaming in his belly. He turns to the douen cowering by my bed, pointing to the soucouyant's skin. "Pick that up and come." The douen jumps, grabbing up its mistress's skin and clothes. Bazil turns to me, his nostrils flaring.

"My little summoner. I suppose now I owe *you* a favor."

I look around my destroyed room. "I don't suppose you can fix all this?"

Bazil snorts again, and snaps his fingers.

I'm at Carnival with my parents, the one they have here in Brooklyn. It's not the same as back home. But the food, the music, the costumes—it's familiar enough. Reminds me that even if I'm becoming American, this is still part of me too.

"Nice Jab."

The words fill my head with flashes of Miss Marabella. But when I spin around, there's a girl. She's my age—in jeans, a T-shirt, and a Bajan flag around her neck. Her brown freckles are even darker than her brown skin, like her frizzy brown hair. What I'm gawking at, though, is what's behind her: a towering figure in bright colorful clothing and a wide hat, with long willowy legs and arms. A Moko Jumbie. Not one of the stilt walkers in the parade—but a *real* Moko Jumbie!

"Nice Moko Jumbie," I reply, hardly believing my eyes.

The girl grins. "I'm Cheryl. We saw your Jab. Thought we'd say hi."

"We?"

She motions to several other kids in the crowd, each with a spirit!

"The tall girl is Patsey. She's from the Bahamas and that big bird-thingy is her Chickcharnie. Devin is the one with glasses. His Bacoo—the little pointy-eared man eating a banana—followed him from Guyana. That last one is Kelvin, from Georgia. His Boo Hag looks scary, with all those teeth, but she won't bite—much. We have a sorta secret club at school. You'll be there tomorrow, right? I'll introduce you—if you'd like."

I nod. "I'd like that a lot! Wait. What kind of secret club?"

She leans in to whisper. "There's monsters in this city. Did you know? We try to hunt them down, before they hurt people. You okay with that?"

I smile so wide, it hurts.

We walk over to the others, who wave at me. My Jab follows, dancing down Eastern Parkway with a Moko Jumbie—bits of memory and magic that we brought with us to this new place, and that we can't help but hold on to.

MY DAD SAYS THAT SOME PEOPLE DON'T WANT TO SEE MY JOY.

I WISH THAT WASN'T TRUE...

BUT WHEN YOU LOOK AT BOOKS AND MOVIES AND STUFF...

THEY MAKE YOU THINK THAT KIDS LIKE ME ARE *ALWAYS* ANGRY...

OR SAD...

LIKE WE'RE THE *ONLY* ONES WHO EVER FEEL THAT WAY...

BUT IT'S NOT JUST US. *EVERYONE* IS SAD OR MAD SOMETIMES.

RIGHT?

EMBRACING MY **BLACK BOY JOY**

by Jerry Craft

THESE SAME EYES THAT GET ALL TEARY WHEN I'M SAD . . .
ALSO SEE ALL THE BEAUTIFUL THINGS AROUND ME.
BUT THERE'S NO MOVIE ABOUT THAT.
DAD SAYS WE HAVE TO MAKE OUR OWN MOVIES . . .
TO SHOW THE WORLD THAT THE SAME MOUTHS THAT POUT WHEN WE'RE ANGRY . . .
ALSO KISS OUR MOMS GOOD NIGHT. PEOPLE NEED TO SEE THAT, TOO.
AND ONE DAY . . . ONE OF THESE MOUTHS "THAT ONLY FROWN" JUST MIGHT GIVE A SPEECH THAT WILL CHANGE THE WORLD.
BUT THERE AREN'T MANY BOOKS ABOUT *THAT* EITHER.
SO I GUESS WE NEED TO WRITE OUR OWN BOOKS.

THE LIFE I WANT FOR ME IS THE LIFE I WANT FOR ALL KIDS LIKE ME.
I WANT OUR EARS TO HEAR SO MANY GOOD THINGS THAT THEY GET ALL FILLED UP.
WOULDN'T THAT BE COOL?
AND FOR OUR HANDS TO ALWAYS BE HAPPY HOLDING TOYS . . .
OR PETTING DOGS . . .
OR BUILDING GREAT THINGS-
EVEN WHEN WE'RE BIG!

AND I WANT US TO
SHARE OUR JOY, TOO.

ARMS THAT GIVE THE
BEST HUGS *EVER!*

AND LEGS THAT KNOW THEY
CAN DO MORE THAN JUST
SOAR ABOVE THE RIM.

LEGS THAT SOAR
ACROSS
THE STAGE.

OR LEGS THAT WILL STAND TOGETHER
TO MAKE SURE OTHERS HAVE
JOY IN THEIR LIVES, TOO.

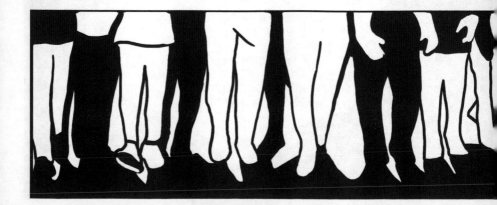

THE GRIOT OF GROVER STREET

BY KWAME MBALIA

PART THREE

FORT LAY on the floor, galaxies swirling beneath him, and clasped his hands behind his head. Mr. G did the same. The two stared up at the giant jar now filled to the brim with humming, melodious bubbles of joy. It filled the Between with a soft blue light, and planets, stars, comets, and asteroids swirled slowly around it.

"You see?" Mr. G said softly. "Joy is at the center of everything. Just have to coax it out."

Fort squinted. "It's like a galaxy of goodness."

"More like a spectacular solar system."

"A constellation of contentment."

Mr. G held up a fist and Fort dapped it. They stared at the jar for a few more minutes, and then Fort sighed. "I guess this means we're done here."

Mr. G nodded. "Just about."

Fort sat up and clutched his knees to his chest. "I like

it here. It's like . . . gardening, but for joy. In space. So actually it's nothing like gardening."

A small planet floated out of orbit and bobbed gently toward them. Mr. G watched it, then groaned as he pulled himself to his feet. "Looks like this is your stop, young Fortitude. You're needed. The job must be finished."

The planet floated to a stop in front of them. Fort, confused, stood to get a closer look. When he stepped forward, the planet shimmered, stretched, and twisted! It grew larger and wider, until finally it loomed over him, a giant silver rectangle.

"It's another door," he said, staring in wonder.

Mr. G nodded. "Back to your world. To the very spot where we departed, in fact."

The door opened. Bright Carolina sunlight fell through. After spending so much time in the Between, Fort was nearly blinded. But strangely, he found himself eager to get back. No one would ever believe where he'd been, but that didn't matter, not really. Having a secret only he could remember, an experience designed just for him . . . well, it was like a friend that would always travel by his side.

Fort stepped closer to the doorway, then turned to look back at Mr. G. "What about you? Are you going back to the Between? Maybe I could . . . come back and visit? If that's okay with you," he hurried to add.

The old man sighed. "I would like nothing more, but I think this is it for me, young Fortitude. Carrying the jar of joy, maintaining the vastness of the Between . . . it's grown to be too much. I'm tired. Once you leave I think I shall pick a nice planet and find a little joy for myself while I still can."

Fort shook his head in confusion. "You're retiring? But . . . what about the joy? Who will collect it? And you still have to deliver the jar! What about the balance? Who's going to restore the balance?"

Mr. G smiled. He pulled something out of his pocket and tossed it over. Fort caught it and froze.

It was a key ring.

"I think I'm leaving the Between in good hands," Mr. G said softly.

Fort spluttered, shook his head. Him? Run the Between? Collect joy and maintain balance? He didn't know the first thing about it! Well, yes, he knew how to collect the joy now. How to sift out memories of loved ones, of first crushes, of hitting the right dance move at the right time and hearing friends cheer. He knew how to snag the feelings of contentment, of growth, of love. Mr. G had showed him. But doing it on his own? He couldn't.

Could he?

"What about," Fort asked, still in a daze, "what

about the delivery? I don't even know where it goes. I don't know who needs it!"

The smile on Mr. G's face, impossibly, grew even wider as he pointed to the doorway. "Don't you?"

Fort stared at him, confused. He turned. Through the bright sunlight shining in the doorway, across the gleaming blacktop parking lot with the freshly painted yellow lines, past the somber sign advertising Aunt Netta's repast, up the stairs of Grover Street Church, Fort watched the front doors burst open and several adults in suits and dresses—church members!—run out in a flurry.

"Something's wrong," he said.

Mr. G stretched and began a set of weird kicks where he tried to touch his heel to the back of his head. "On the contrary, young Fortitude. I suspect something is *very* right."

"But there's Mr. Richards, and Mrs. Jeffers and her sister, and—"

Fort broke off. Swallowed. Took two steps forward before he even realized he was walking. Stared at the pregnant woman moving slowly down the stairs, her hand on her belly as the others fluttered around her. Suddenly he knew.

"Mama," he whispered. "She's gonna have the baby."

A hand landed gently on his shoulder. Mr. G nodded

at Fort's mother, who walked slowly by the homegoing sign. "It's like I said. Balance. Where there's death, there will be life. Where there used to be emptiness"—he tapped Fort's hand holding the keys—"there will be purpose. And where there is sadness, there will be joy. If someone is unable to find it themself, like . . . oh, I don't know, a newborn baby . . . well, someone else should help them, right? Now. Here you are."

Fort turned. Mr. G held out the handle of the wagon, the jar of joy glowing in back. "I told you, my boy. I'm getting too old for this. Time for someone new to search the Between for those in desperate need of joy. And what better place to start . . . than right at home?"

Fort took the handle, still in shock. He was going to be a big brother. He was going to be a . . . wizard?

Mr. G turned and walked slowly back into the darkness, fingers grazing the stars.

Fort licked his lips. "How do I know who needs joy?" he shouted after the old man.

"Easy!" came the reply. "We all do!"

Fort took a deep breath and turned to face the doorway. His mother waited on the curb, probably for someone to bring around the car. Soon they'd be on their way to the hospital. Soon he'd have another person in the family, someone tiny and precious and unable to fend for themself. Whoever his sibling turned out to be, they would be born into a tough world. A sometimes-sad world, where people you loved died, got hurt, or even just felt blue from time to time. They would need joy. They would need Fort.

Fortitude Jones squared his shoulders. He squeezed the handle of the wagon, lifted his chin, and nodded. He had a job to do.

One step.

Two.

And he walked through the doorway, wagon trundling behind him, as the newest, youngest, and just-a-teeny-tiny-bit-scarediest Griot of Grover Street.

ACKNOWLEDGMENTS

Deep inhale

Always thank the village, because you can't do it alone.

Thank you to everyone who made this possible: from my agent, Patrice Caldwell, to Hannah Hill at Delacorte Press/Penguin Random House, to the sixteen authors who joined me in sharing their joy: B.B., DaVaun, Dean, Don, George, Jason, Jay, Jerry, Julian R., Julian W., Justin, Lamar, Phenderson, Suyi, Tochi, and Varian. Thanks for riding with me, fam.

Big thanks to Kadir Nelson for the dope cover.

Huge thanks to everyone behind the scenes working so furiously to bring you this joy: Beverly Horowitz, Barbara Marcus, Dominique Cimina, Kristopher Kam, John Adamo, Tamar Schwartz, Jenica Nasworthy, Colleen Fellingham, Alison Kolani, April Ward, and Jen Valero.

Thank you to the boys I grew up with, my brothers, my friends, the ones who ran the streets with me and the ones who couldn't escape them. Thank you to my Howard U boys, who still hold me down, twenty years strong, I love you all.

Thank you to my wife, who would call me her boy, and at whom I blow a raspberry in return. Take that, love.

Thank you to my girls, my daughters, who know that I would never diminish their stories.

Finally, thank you, reader. I hope this book brought you joy.

ABOUT THE AUTHORS

B. B. ALSTON lives in Lexington, South Carolina. *Amari and the Night Brothers* is his debut middle-grade novel. When he's not writing, he can be found eating too many sweets and exploring country roads to see where they lead.

DEAN ATTA's poems deal with themes of race, gender, and identity. He regularly performs across the UK and internationally, and his work has been shortlisted for the Polari First Book Prize and has appeared on MTV and BET. His debut YA novel, *The Black Flamingo*, is a Stonewall Book Award winner and a CILIP Carnegie Medal Nominee. You can find him online at deanatta.com.

JERRY CRAFT is the *New York Times* bestselling and Newbery Medal–winning author of the graphic novel *New Kid*. His second graphic novel, *Class Act,* was an instant *New York Times* bestseller. Craft is also the creator of *Mama's Boyz,* an award-winning comic strip, which won the African American Literary Award five times. He is a cofounder of the Schomburg Center's Annual Black Comic Book Festival. He received his BFA from the School of Visual Arts.

JAY COLES was born and raised in Indianapolis. He is the author of the critically acclaimed *Tyler Johnson Was Here* and *Things We Couldn't Say,* a composer with the American Society of Composers, Authors, and Publishers, and a professional musician. He is a graduate of Vincennes University and Ball State University and holds degrees in English and Liberal Arts. When he's not writing diverse books, he's advocating for them, traveling the world, gushing over books by his favorite authors, and composing music for various music publishers. Jay writes full-time and currently resides in Muncie, Indiana, which he loves a lot, but he would love the chance to live farther west someday.

 P. DJÉLÌ CLARK is the award-winning and Hugo-, Nebula-, and Sturgeon-nominated author of the novellas *Ring Shout, The Black God's Drums,* and *The Haunting of Tram Car 015.* His short stories have appeared in online venues such as Tor.com, Heroic Fantasy Quarterly, Beneath Ceaseless Skies, and in print anthologies including *Griots, Hidden Youth,* and *Clockwork Cairo.* He is a founding member of *FIYAH: A Magazine of Black Speculative Fiction* and an infrequent reviewer at *Strange Horizons.* He resides in a small

Edwardian castle in New England with his wife, twin daughters, and pet dragon, where he works as an academic historian. When so inclined, he rambles on issues of speculative fiction, politics, and diversity at his aptly named blog The Disgruntled Haradrim. His debut novel is *A Master of Djinn*.

Adrienne Giles

LAMAR GILES writes for teens and adults across multiple genres; his work appears frequently on Best Of lists. He is the author of the acclaimed novels *Fake ID, Endangered, Overturned, Spin, The Last Last-Day-of-Summer, Not So Pure and Simple,* and *The Last Mirror on the Left,* as well as numerous pieces of short fiction. He is a founding member of We Need Diverse Books and resides in Virginia with his wife.

Arin Sang-urai

DON P. HOOPER is a writer and filmmaker of Jamaican heritage. He was a staff writer for the 2017–2020 Writers Guild of America East Awards, and his directing work has been selected and featured in the NYC Horror Film Festival, the New Jersey Horror Con and Film Festival (award winner), Martha's Vineyard African American Film Festival, and others. His poetry has been featured in Unión de Periodistas, the "Ransack" chapbook, and the "Jerk Apricots and Chains" chapbook. He does voice-over in video games and documentaries. He proudly reps Brooklyn, all day, every day.

Sean Howard Photo

GEORGE M. JOHNSON is an award-winning Black Queer writer, author, and activist living in the NYC area. They are the Indie bestselling author of *All Boys Aren't Blue*, a memoir manifesto discussing their young adult experience growing up Black and Queer. George has written on a range of topics for publications such as *Teen Vogue, Entertainment Tonight,* NBC, *The Root, BuzzFeed,* and *Essence.* George also served as Guest Editor for BET.com's Pride month. George has been seen on MSNBC, *BuzzFeed*'s AM2DM, *The Grapevine, PBS Nightly News,* and various shows on Sirius XM Radio. On social media, they have an impressive presence, with over 70,000 engaged followers on Twitter who are always eager to see what George is writing next. George recently signed a deal with Gabrielle Union and Sony TV to develop their memoir for television.

Kenneth Gall

VARIAN JOHNSON is the author of several novels for children and young adults, including *The Parker Inheritance,* which won both Coretta Scott King Author Honor and *Boston Globe–Horn Book* Honor awards; *The Great*

Greene Heist, an ALA-ALSC Notable Children's Book and a Texas Library Association Lone Star List selection; and the graphic novel *Twins,* illustrated by Shannon Wright, which was named a *School Library Journal* Best Book and a *Horn Book* Fanfare Selection. He lives with his family near Austin, Texas. You can visit him on the web at varianjohnson.com and on Twitter at @varianjohnson.

Bryan Jones Photography

KWAME MBALIA is a husband, father, writer, *New York Times* bestselling author, and former pharmaceutical metrologist, in that order. His debut middle-grade novel, *Tristan Strong Punches a Hole in the Sky,* was a Coretta Scott King Honor book and an instant *New York Times* bestseller. Its sequel, *Tristan Strong Destroys the World,* was also an instant *New York Times* bestseller. A Howard University graduate and a Midwesterner now living in North Carolina, Kwame survives on dad jokes and Cheez-Its.

Manuel Ruiz

SUYI DAVIES OKUNGBOWA is a Nigerian author of fantasy, science fiction, and other speculative works inspired by his West African origins. He is the author of *Son of the Storm,* the first novel in the Nameless Republic epic fantasy trilogy. His highly acclaimed debut, the godpunk fantasy novel *David Mogo, Godhunter,* was hailed by *Wired* as "the subgenre's platonic deific ideal." His shorter fiction and essays have appeared internationally on Tor.com and in periodicals such as *Lightspeed, Nightmare, Strange Horizons, Fireside, Podcastle,* and *The Dark* and anthologies like *Year's Best Science Fiction and Fantasy, A World of Horror,* and *People of Colour Destroy Science Fiction.* He has taught creative writing at the University of Arizona (where he also completed his MFA in Creative Writing) as well as spoken and lectured at various venues in the United States and beyond. He currently lives in Tucson, Arizona. You can find him on Twitter at @IAmSuyiDavies and on Instagram at @suyidavies. Learn more at suyidavies.com.

Christina Orlando

TOCHI ONYEBUCHI is the author of *Riot Baby,* which won the New England Book Award for Fiction; *Beasts Made of Night; Crown of Thunder;* and *War Girls,* a Locus Award finalist. He holds degrees from Yale University, New York University's Tisch School of the Arts, Columbia Law School, and Sciences Po. His short fiction has appeared in *Asimov's Science Fiction, Omenana Magazine, Black Enough: Stories of Being Young & Black in America,* and elsewhere.

His nonfiction has appeared on Tor.com and in the *Harvard Journal of African American Public Policy,* among other places. His most recent novel is *Rebel Sisters.*

Afaq

JULIAN RANDALL is a Queer Black poet from Chicago. He has received fellowships from Cave Canem, CantoMundo, Callaloo, BOAAT, Tin House, Milkweed Editions, and the Watering Hole. Julian is the recipient of a Pushcart Prize. Julian is also the winner of the Betty Berzon Emerging Writer Award from the Publishing Triangle and of the Frederick Bock Prize. His poetry has been published in the *New York Times Magazine, Ploughshares,* and POETRY and anthologized in *The Breakbeat Poets Vol. 4, Nepantla,* and *Furious Flower.* He has essays in *Vibe, Black Nerd Problems,* and other venues. He holds an MFA in poetry from Ole Miss. He is the author of *Refuse,* winner of the Cave Canem Poetry Prize and a finalist for an NAACP Image Award, and of the middle-grade novel *Pilar Ramirez and the Prison of Zafa*. He talks a lot about poems and other things on Twitter at @JulianThePoet.

Dayo Kosoko

JASON REYNOLDS is an award-winning and #1 *New York Times* bestselling author. Jason's many books include *Miles Morales: Spider-Man;* the Track series (*Ghost, Patina, Sunny,* and *Lu*); *Long Way Down,* which received a Newbery Honor, a Printz Honor, and a Coretta Scott King Honor; and *Look Both Ways,* which was a National Book Award Finalist. His latest book, *Stamped: Racism, Antiracism, and You,* is a collaboration with Ibram X. Kendi. Jason is the 2020–2021 National Ambassador for Young People's Literature and has appeared on *The Daily Show with Trevor Noah,*

Late Night with Seth Meyers,
and *CBS This Morning.* He is on
faculty at Lesley University, for the
Writing for Young People MFA
Program, and lives in Washington,
DC. You can find his ramblings at
JasonWritesBooks.com.

JUSTIN A. REYNOLDS has always
wanted to be a writer. *Opposite of
Always,* his debut YA novel, was an
Indies Introduce Top Ten Debut and
a *School Library Journal* Best Book
of the Year, was translated into
nineteen languages, and is being
developed for film by Paramount
Players. His second YA novel, *Early
Departures,* was a *Kirkus Reviews*
Best Teen Book of the Year. justin
is also the cofounder of the CLE
Reads Book Festival, a Cleveland
Book Festival for middle-grade
and young adult writers, which he
launched in July 2019. He hangs
out in northeast Ohio with his

family and is probably somewhere, right now, dancing terribly. That, or maybe sportsing.

DAVAUN SANDERS resides in Phoenix. His short fiction has been published by *FIYAH: Magazine of Black Speculative Fiction*, PodCastle, Broken Eye Books, Dancing Star Press, and others. He currently serves as executive editor for the World Fantasy Award–winning and two-time Hugo Award–nominated *FIYAH*. His most recent editorial project is *Breathe FIYAH*, a flash fiction anthology collaboration with Tor.com. He hopes to continue expanding his body of work in children's fiction, for his own twins and for kids everywhere who deserve to enjoy inclusive stories. Follow him on Twitter and Instagram at @davaunsanders.

JULIAN WINTERS is the award-winning author of *Running With Lions,* which won an IBPA Benjamin Franklin Gold Award, as well as *How to Be Remy Cameron* and *The Summer of Everything.* A self-proclaimed comic book geek, Julian lives in Decatur, Georgia, where he can be found watching the only two sports he can follow: volleyball and soccer. Visit him online at julianwinters.com.